He Was Her Husband—and Her Master!

'My wishes are not to be ignored, Martine. You must learn that when I say a thing I mean it.'

Her chin lifted. 'I won't be dictated to, Luke! There is no harm in my talking to Kelvin.'

'I was not speaking about harm but about my wishes. You will keep away from this man, do you understand? In Greece, the husband is the master. The sooner you accept this the better it will be for you.'

She paled with anger. How could she convince him that he could not dominate her?

ANNE HAMPSON
currently makes her home in England, but this top romance author has travelled and lived all over the world. This variety of experience is reflected in her books, which present the ever-changing face of romance as it is found wherever people fall in love.

Dear Reader:

Silhouette Books is pleased to announce the creation of a new line of contemporary romances—*Silhouette Special Editions*. Each month we'll bring you six new love stories written by the best of today's authors—Janet Dailey, Brooke Hastings, Laura Hardy, Sondra Stanford, Linda Shaw, Patti Beckman, and many others.

Silhouette Special Editions are written with American women in mind; they are for readers who want more: more story, more details and descriptions, more realism, and more *romance*. *Special Editions* are longer than most contemporary romances allowing for a closer look at the relationship between hero and heroine with emphasis on heightened romantic tension and greater sensuous and sensual detail. If you want more from a romance, be sure to look for *Silhouette Special Editions* on sale this February wherever you buy books.

We welcome any suggestions or comments, and I invite you to write us at the address below.

Karen Solem
Editor-in-Chief
Silhouette Books
P.O. Box 769
New York, N. Y. 10019

ANNE HAMPSON
Realm of the Pagans

Silhouette *Romance*

Published by Silhouette Books New York

America's Publisher of Contemporary Romance

SILHOUETTE BOOKS, a Simon & Schuster Division of
GULF & WESTERN CORPORATION
1230 Avenue of the Americas, New York, N.Y. 10020

ISBN: 0-671-57128-1

First Silhouette Books printing January, 1982

10 9 8 7 6 5 4 3 2 1

Other Silhouette Romances by Anne Hampson

Chapter One

The darkness was ghastly, creating monsters of the mountains and bringing them so close that Martine felt smothered within the confines of the car, and wished with all her heart that she had not succumbed to the impulsive desire to get away from her fiancé.

Her fiancé . . . ? Until a couple of hours ago he was her fiancé . . . but now . . . ?

Tears began to sting her eyes, impairing her vision so that driving became even more difficult.

'He didn't mean it!' she cried aloud. 'He couldn't have! It's only infatuation he feels for Sophia! He's flattered by her attention and—and —perhaps he thinks of her fortune—just a little. It would be natural. Dear Kelvin, come after me! I said where I was going—to Athens, so you know this is the road I would take. Please come to me—*please!*'

She and Kelvin had begun as boss and secretary. He was an author, having written several books on archaeology. Martine had always been interested in archaeology and was, in fact, a member of the Archaelogical Society in England. She had spent most week-ends helping to unearth a Roman theatre near her home town of Warrencester, in the Midlands. Kelvin, naturally interested in the recent find, had visited the site and within a month had tempted Martine to work for him, in spite of the fact that she had an excellent post already. The truth was that Kelvin had attracted her from the moment she set eyes on him—standing there, tall and handsome, his whole attention on the work that was taking place. It was done almost entirely by students from the nearby university or people like Martine who, like the students, were willling to give their services free; the joy of discovery being reward enough for the work they put in.

Martine had been working for Kelvin only a few weeks when after finishing his present book, he announced his intention of writing about Olympia in Greece. Thrilled with the idea of visiting the famous site of the ancient Games, Martine had rented out her flat, packed what she would need and was ready to go immediately when Kelvin had asked.

And on the plane going over to Athens he had proposed to her. . . .

Life was so good. She felt as if she were floating on a star as the plane hovered above the clouds, sunlit clouds, silver clouds with no shadows visible or even contemplated. Then from nowhere—or so it seemed—appeared Sophia, lovely young daughter of Andreas Sotiris, wealthy exporter of wine and the owner of vast acreage in other parts of Greece. Sophia had been away at school in Athens but after finishing her education, she had returned home. It seemed that even at their first meeting Kelvin was fascinated by the dark beauty of the Greek girl. Yes, Martine thought as she drove the car along the perilous road with its twists and turns, its narrowness and its weather-worn surfaces unexpectedly making the car behave as if it were on tires of steel instead of rubber, the girl possessed a beauty which would attract any man. She was young, unsophisticated . . . but Martine guessed she was clever for all that, and unscrupulous. She had wanted Kelvin; she had made no attempt to ignore his interest; on the contrary, she had encouraged it. Yet Martine had never even suspected her fiancé of developing any deep feelings for the girl. He was kind to her, friendly, because her father was their neighbour and he had allowed them to use a small villa in the grounds of his house. It was divided into two separate apartments so it had been ideal for Martine and her fiancé—they were close but yet their sleeping quarters were respectably separate.

The road became narrower than ever and for a few minutes Martine's whole attention was on her driving. And then, just as thoughts and regrets and hopes began to take possession of her mind again, the car jerked and spluttered. Then she found herself pressing the accelerator in a futile attempt to get the engine purring again. With her heart lurching she came to a silent halt, and slid out into the blanket of darkness where not even the sound of a night bird could be heard. Shivering with incomprehensible fear, she just stood, her mind half dazed by what was happening to her. Fate was against her, she decided, wondering if she would be here until daylight, or if by some remote chance another car would come along. It must be almost midnight. . . . She must have been mad to pack a bag and run from Kelvin like that! Only now did she realise that her optimism had been so great that she had been sure he would come after her in the big Mercedes he had bought on coming to Greece a few weeks ago.

What must she do? Begin to walk . . . ? Suddenly her thoughts braked and her heart leapt. Headlights! It must be Kelvin. He was sorry, contrite, guilty. He had come after her and now everything was going to be all right!

She stood in the middle of the road and waved her arms, then stepped back. Yes, it was the Merc! And so positive was she that the tall dark shadow coming from the car was, in fact, her fiancé that without hesitation she ran forward and flung herself into his arms.

'Oh, darling—I knew you would come! I shouldn't have run away—' She lifted her face in the darkness and, rising on tiptoe, pressed her eager lips to his. For one astonished second there was no response and then Martine felt the sensuous lips part and she was stunned by the passion in her fiancé's kiss. How contrite he must be to kiss her with such ardour! Never before had he shown such enthusiasm. He had been loving and gentle, yes, but without this show of passion, this new approach which made it seem he had had years of experience with women. She pressed close, putting her arms about his neck, thrusting her fingers into his hair. . . .

Kelvin's hair was soft and fine; this hair was strong and wiry. . . . She leant away, her eyes trying to probe the dimness.

'That was as delightful as it was unexpected,' drawled a faintly accented voice. 'My name's Loukas Leoros. What's yours?'

'I—I—' Hot with embarrassment, Martine wrenched herself free of the strong hands that held her. 'I th–thought you were—were my fiancé,' she stammered. 'His car is the same make—I saw the shape and concluded . . . ' Her voice trailed away to silence as she realised that this stranger, this Greek, would not want to hear her explanation. 'Will you give me a lift to—to wherever you are going, please? My car's broken down.'

'So it would seem. You were expecting your fiancé to come?' She said nothing and after a moment he added, a curious inflection in his voice, 'You've quarrelled and you ran away? Just like a woman to expect her man to follow, pandering to her perversity.' His tone was cynical and faintly contemptuous. Yet there was a certain pleasantry about it that scared Martine because she knew the reputation of the Greeks . . . and she was undoubtedly in the most vulnerable situation possible. He could do her any injury and get away with it, she thought. And then suddenly, expectedly, the moon emerged from the blackness of the clouds, spreading its silver effulgence across the landscape, lighting up the road to reveal the features of the man whose presence was bringing Martine both relief and fear. She saw a face of remarkable distinction, with nobility its chief characteristic. She found herself recalling the statues in the Athens Museum—statues of pagan gods and heroes, their faces severe and classical; ruthless, vigorous lines adding to the overall impression of severity and mastery. Masters of everything—and everyone—that came their way. This man—Loukas Leoros—might have inspired the sculptors of ancient Greece, might have been a throwback, she thought. But whereas the statues depicted handsome, unscarred beauty, this man wore a scar down the left side of his face—not too noticeable in this pale silver light, but there all the same. Otherwise, though, he was indisputably good-looking, and she guessed his age to be around thirty. Were his eyes really black, she wondered, or was it merely the lack of proper light which made them appear so? His nose was straight, his mouth full-lipped and sensual, typically Greek. He differed from most Greeks, though, because he was tall—well over six feet, she estimated, comparing his height with that of Kelvin—and there was not an ounce of unnecessary weight on his lithe and upright frame. His hair, thick and black and wiry was inclined to wave on each side of the widow's peak, a feature which seemed to give him a decidedly satanic look. She shivered involuntarily, allowing her imagination to run away with her as she saw herself being molested by this man.

'Will you give me a lift?' she requested again, ignoring his comments and inserting a gentle plea into her voice, as if by so doing she could gain his sympathy so that he would feel he could not molest her. She looked up into the austere countenance and something stirred within her as a smile came slowly to his lips.

'Don't be afraid of me,' he said quietly. And then, 'Where have you left this fiancé of yours?'

'In Olympia. We live there.'

'Olympia?' in some surprise. 'What are you

doing there? Is this fiancé of yours English or Greek?'

'English.' She paused a moment. 'He was my employer before we became engaged,' she explained, feeling that the man's intent stare was an invitation for her to confide. 'We quarrelled, as you surmised, and I came away—with only one suitcase,' she ended absurdly and heard her companion laugh.

'If he has any sense he'll beat you when he gets you back,' he commented, lifting a lean brown hand to stifle a yawn. 'I know I should.'

Martine's blue eyes glinted.

'If you would be so kind—'

'—as to give you a lift? I feel I ought to take you back to this fiancé of yours. He's probably worried out of his mind,' he added with a sort of satirical disdain. 'More fool him. He should know you will come running back eventually. They all do—'

'Mr. Leoros,' interrupted Martine coldly, 'you need not bother about the lift! I can sit in the car until the morning when another car is sure to come along!'

'Probably containing an amorous Greek who will rape you and then drive away. Get into my car and I'll drive you back to Olympia.'

'I don't want—'

'In, I said,' he cut her off imperiously and with the added encouragement of a little push. 'I see you managed to pull your car off the road so there'll be no danger to anyone who might just be driving this way.'

Once in the car Martine leant back, amazed to find herself so relaxed. But on thinking about it as they drove, her companion looking for a place to turn around, she concluded that her state of mind resulted from relief that she had not met with a situation that could have had dire results. This man was obviously honourable—perhaps happily married, or engaged and so not interested in any other woman.

'What's the address?' he wanted to know when eventually they entered the outskirts of the sacred site.

'We live in a villa in the grounds of Mr. Sotiris's house. Do you happen to know him?'

A small and inexplicable silence followed before her companion spoke. 'Yes, I do know him—very well, in fact.'

'So you know where to drop me, then?'

'The villa's at the back of his house?'

'That's right.' There were two villas, one of which was facing the road and it was occupied by the head gardener.

'Your fiancé lives in the same house as you?'

'It's divided into two apartments.'

'Do you know Mr. Sotiris well?' he inquired curiously.

'I haven't spoken to him above half-a-dozen times.' A small pause and then, as if driven on by some compulsion she could not conquer, 'He has a very young and beautiful daughter, Sophia.'

'Correct.' Fleetingly he slid her a glance, noticing the golden hair, long and straight, flicked up attractively at the ends, the strong yet attractively feminine lines and curves of her face, the full generous mouth, the high, intelligent forehead. 'What made you mention Sophia?'

'I don't quite know,' with well-feigned indifference which apparently lacked the effect she wanted.

'She's after every man she sees. Could I make

an intelligent guess and say you mentioned her because she was on your mind—because she has come between you and your fiancé?'

Martine remained silent for a space, aware that she was not too surprised by the assumption which Loukas Leoros had made. That he was a highly-intelligent man was plain; that he was keenly perceptive was also obvious. Martine found herself wondering about him, what he did for a living, about his family and his life generally. Stupid thoughts because he was a mere stranger who had been kind enough to come to her rescue. She heard herself say, slowly and reluctantly, 'She has come between us, yes. Kelvin seems infatuated with her . . .'

'And so you tackled him and you quarrelled?'

'It was more serious than a quarrel,' she admitted. 'Kelvin said it was all ended between him and me. I—I gave him h–his ring b–back—' To her consternation she burst into tears. 'I'm s–sorry. . . .'

He stopped the car just beyond the entrance to the gates of the Sanctuary. Martine put a handkerchief to her eyes and dried them, blinking as the interior light was switched on.

'Are you quite sure he is worth it?' The foreign voice was faintly harsh, the accent rather more pronounced than she had heard it before.

'I love him,' was her simple reply and she heard a swift intake of breath before Loukas Leoros spoke.

'He obviously doesn't love you.'

'He did at one time.'

'And now you have lost your job as well as your fiancé.' A statement which seemed once and for all to make Martine accept that the affair really was ended. She felt angry with this man because he had the power to convince her, for up till now hope had still flourished deep in her heart.

'I suppose so.' Her eyes strayed to the sacred grove that lay so peacefully in the hollow of the tree-clothed hills. The clouds had all dispersed by now and the moon was full and high over the sacred precincts, its argent glow giving the temple columns a somewhat ghostly appearance. She could faintly hear the murmuring of the river above the chirping of cicadas and the silvery music made by the sheep bells on the hillsides. So peaceful! Olympia, where all feuds were forgotten during the Games, where in ancient times all man's effort went into the glory of sport rather than the more doubtful glory of slaying his enemies. Perhaps one day the peoples of the world would make a universal shrine of this place . . . and all wars would become the horrors of the past.

'What are you thinking?' The voice was soft, yet it carried an imperious ring which demanded a truthful answer. It came easily but with a sigh as Martine spoke aloud the thoughts and ideas that had been passing through her mind.

'It's fanciful, of course,' she ended and her companion agreed, which was depressing and the ready tears misted her eyes again. 'Life is rotten!' she exclaimed. 'I would not care if I knew I was going to die!'

'Yes you would. This will pass and you'll meet someone else.'

'You say that but your voice has a cynical ring.'

'I have no faith in love between a man and a woman.'

'But that's silly. Love is what makes a marriage, and—'

'Here in Greece many marriages are arranged. Where does love come into it?'

'In the West we marry for love.'

'You do? What is love? Can you define it for me?' His tone was edged with amusement and contempt. Martine concluded he was not married, nor was he likely to be. A born bachelor who was obviously content with his way of life. She suspected he had had many pillow friends, and he was young enough to have many more.

'Love is caring so deeply for someone that you'd die for them.'

'Men have died for their countries. That's loyalty, not love.'

'Loyalty and love are kin.'

'Kin, perhaps, but not one and the same.' He shook his head. 'Love is a fallacy—a state of mind invented by the female of our species who, unfortunately, were provided with romantic fantasies unknown to men—'

'Oh, no! I can't agree!'

He turned to her; she saw the mocking curve of his lips and frowned inwardly. 'Have you ever known a man to be in love—as you call it?'

'Kelvin. . . .'

'Was never in love with you.' He looked at her intently, his eyes moving over her face—tear-stained but lovely—then to her throat and the delicate slope of her shoulders, then lower to the alluring, tantalising curve of her firm, young breasts. She coloured at his examination; he was stripping her. She felt he was actually fondling her. . . . Her colour deepened and, without warning, he took her in his arms, turned her face with a firm hand gripping her chin, and then his lips were claiming hers in a kiss so ardent and sensual that she had no strength to protest. In fact, she was soon reciprocating, thrilling to the moist probing, the mastery which compelled her to part her lips, and she quivered with a totally new and exquisite emotion as she felt the roughness of his tongue caressing her own. It was only when his hand enclosed her breast that she shied away, ashamed and blushing, pulling the edges of her thin white cardigan together.

'Why waste your tears on a man who cares nothing for you. Be my pillow friend and have all that life has to offer.'

'Your—!' She stared at his profile disbelievingly. 'What kind of man are you? Do you pick up any woman and go to bed with her?'

She had not known what to expect but certainly she hadn't envisaged the cruel grip that caused her to wince and then cry out in pain and protest.

'How dare you speak to me like that!' he said harshly. 'I do *not* pick up women!'

'But you picked me up,' she protested, tugging at her wrist and merely succeeding in giving herself more pain.

'I came to your aid,' he corrected, still in that harsh and angry tone. 'And you appeal to me. I suppose I am sorry for you in your distress—'

'I don't believe you,' she broke in hotly. 'You merely desire me, as so many Greek men desire women they see. Well, I'm not so cheap—get that!' She made to open the door but her wrist was still tightly held and she knew she could not get out of the car.

'I shall give you a ring tomorrow.' And he let go of her wrist then, and started the car. 'I suppose you do have a phone in your apartment?'

'Yes, there is one, but I won't have you phoning me. I'm grateful for your help—very grateful that you would trouble to turn back and bring me home, but that is the end of it as far as I am concerned. Besides, you must live some distance from here?' She ended on a questioning note, looking at his profile.

'I live in the white villa on the hill,' he told her quietly. 'The one you see so plainly from the Sanctuary—in fact, my main view is directly down on to it.'

'The Villa Cladeos?' she said in some surprise. 'But you were going the other way.'

'I was merely going for a drive. I sometimes do, especially when I have a business problem I want to think out. Night driving's conducive to clear, logical thought.'

Martine did not ask why, but remarked instead that his view must be wonderful. To be able to look down on to the sacred precincts of Olympia. . . .

'I had the house built purposefully for the view.'

True to his word Loukas phoned her the following day. She had been up just over an hour when the ringing brought her from the kitchen where she had been making toast and coffee.

'I told you not to ring,' she began, when he interrupted her to say, 'People do not tell me what to do and what not to do, Martine. I want to see you today. An hour from now?'

Something strange and yet not unpleasant touched her heart. 'I do not want to see you, either in an hour or anytime!'

'What did Kelvin have to say about your running away?'

'I haven't seen him.'

'No?' in some surprise. 'But surely, if you're living so close, you must have seen one another?'

'He was in bed last night—'

'In bed, and knowing you were out in the car, on those lonely and dangerous roads?'

Martine ignored that. 'He must have gone out early this morning. He said yesterday that he was going to Athens to see the curator of the museum there, so perhaps he chose today to do it. I don't really know.'

'Well, I expect you're fully convinced that you and he have no future together. I shall be around in an hour—or perhaps a little earlier.' And without giving her any further chance to protest he replaced the receiver. Martine's mouth tightened. He was certainly persistent!

She thought at first that the best way to deter him would be to look drab and uninteresting when he arrived. But, driven by some hand other than her own, she dressed carefully, donning a white cotton dress trimmed with a flowered border round the hem, and with a similar feature forming a belt below a tight-fitting bodice and above a daintily flared skirt which, though hiding her curves, in fact, accentuated her slenderness. She brushed her hair till it shone, noticing as she stared at herself in the mirror that the tints of tawny brown, so soft and attractive, had not disappeared altogether when her hair was bleached by the hot Grecian sun. Dainty sandals revealed pink-tipped toes below perfectly-shaped ankles and slender legs browned by the outdoor life Martine had led since coming to Greece.

Loukas arrived within five minutes of her being ready and the first words he uttered after she had invited him in were, 'So you did want me to come despite the protests.' His eyes were lazy as they travelled over her—lazy and mocking. And she felt uncomfortable in the extreme even while she freely admitted to the pull of his attraction which sent feathery ripples along her spine.

Without answering she led the way into a cool sitting-room where the zephyr of a breeze ballooned the embroidered net drapes and at the same time carried in the heady scent of flowers. Martine had a bowl of red roses on the table and another of magenta bougainvillaea on the windowsill. She invited her visitor to sit down but he went to the window instead and stood looking out, his eyes trained on the big imposing villa that belonged to Sophia's father. Watching him, Martine felt that had she been able to see his expression it would have been harsh, to say the least. He turned, as if aware of her gaze, and she saw again that lazy, mocking look as his dark eyes slid over her. The scar seemed more pronounced than she expected it to be; she fell to wondering how he had come by it. But she did not ask, naturally. She merely said, adopting an air of cool affability, 'Why are you here, Mr. Leoros?'

'I wanted to see you. I have a proposition to put to you.'

'Yes?' with a tingling of nerves as she waited for him to repeat his invitation of last night.

'Will you marry me?'

She gaped, the room spinning around her so

that she was forced towards a chair, grasping the back for support.

"Wh–what did you say?'

'Need I repeat it?' The delayed smile, the deliberation of the one short sentence, the smooth and casual manner in which he lifted a hand to hide a yawn . . . all these sent Martine into a flurry of sensations that precluded any possibility of clear thought. She sank into the chair, staring up at him as if he had taken leave of his senses. Yet she knew without any doubt at all that he was serious!

'I don't understand you,' she said and the tone was one of complaint, which had the affect of broadening his smile.

'My question was plain enough—nothing cryptic about it.'

'Certainly it's cryptic! You haven't even mentioned a reason for asking it!'

'You're confused,' he said in a softer voice, 'which is only natural. However, my reasons need not trouble you.' He paused, watching her shake her head in bewilderment. After a small pause during which she did not speak, he continued, 'As for you—well, marriage to me would solve all your problems; it would also afford you the satisfaction of knowing you had—er—got your own back on your fiancé—No, do not interrupt!' he went on authoritatively when she opened her mouth. 'No matter what you were about to say, revenge *is* sweet!'

Another pause, and as she looked at his expression Martine found herself shivering. Revenge is sweet. . . . Suddenly she felt she knew why he wanted to marry her. It was for revenge on someone else. But who? A woman who had let him down? He had said quite categorically, though, that he did not believe in love. Therefore, he could not have been hurt because he had never been in love. Or had he . . . ?

Two people who had been let down. . . . It seemed almost natural that they might get together. She frowned, unable to understand her feelings and her thoughts. She had no intention of marrying anyone! If it couldn't be Kelvin then it would be no other man, for she loved him with all her heart.

'I cannot possibly marry you,' she stated at length. 'The idea's preposterous.'

'I don't agree.' He moved towards her and before she realised his intention she was on her feet, brought against his lithe body and, although she struggled, her efforts to free herself were not only puny, but laughable. He held her easily with one arm about her, hawser strong, while his other hand tilted her chin in the most proprietorial manner and the verbal protest she was about to make never even left her lips.

Breathless when at last he drew his mouth from hers, she could only stare and cling to him, for she felt weak from the ardent hunger of his kisses, from the possessive way he had held her, compelling her to meld her soft young body with the virile hardness of his own, making her aware of the new emotion he could arouse within her . . . the desire she had never known before. Her breathing continued to be erratic, while he quickly became calm, his mocking eyes matching the curve of those sensuous lips. She should have been feeling angry, resentful . . . but instead she wanted him to coerce her again, to demand that she reciprocate his love-making.

'You're delightful,' murmured Loukas, his

mouth cool and moist against her cheek. 'We shall do famously together—'

'No—!'

'Yes,' he broke in suavely. 'You're a very sexy young lady, although you haven't realised it until now—Yes, I believe you have realised it but, of course, with the usual female perversity, you'll not admit it.' He laughed then, softly, and Martine wanted to hit him. 'As I was saying, you're a very sexy young lady and you need a man who can satisfy that—'

'Stop it!' Sheer fury looked out of her eyes. 'You're insulting me!'

'The truth can never be an insult, my dear, and I only speak the truth. Think about it. . . .' He bent his head and once again she experienced kisses which she could not resist. And as the passionate moments stretched she became drawn into a vortex of primitive love-making that drew a total response from her . . . and a near surrender. She had wound her arms about his neck, had arched her body in a search for the knowledge of his desire and need for her. His ardour had generated heat within her body; her pulses had throbbed with the desperate longing he had awakened. Shame and self-disgust fought against the urge for complete surrender and she was honest enough to admit that, if Loukas had continued, surrender would have been her lot. 'Well. . . .' Loukas held her from him, a pulse pounding in his temple. 'Have you thought about it?'

'I can't marry you!' she cried fiercely. 'I *won't* marry you!'

Loukas bent and this time his kiss was gentle, without passion or temptation. He released her almost immediately. 'Dine with me this evening,' he said. 'I shall call for you around half past seven.' He was at the door, one hand on the knob. 'Wear a long dress. I want to see what you look like in one.'

'Who do you think you are giving orders to?' she demanded, still fighting to regain full control, still unable to breathe evenly.

'Do as I say and don't ask absurd questions.' He opened the door. 'You desire me just as much as I desire you,' he told her. 'Admit it and make your decision.'

'At first you wanted me for your pillow friend,' she could not help reminding him.

'But you refused, and I realised you would continue to refuse. That is one reason for my asking you to marry me. There is another reason—'

'You want to be revenged on someone?'

He seemed faintly startled but soon recovered. His voice was carelessly suave as he said, nodding his head slightly, 'Yes, I want to be revenged on someone. So that makes two of us with that desire.'

'Please don't call here this evening. I shall not dine with you—not tonight or any other night.'

'I shall call at half past seven.' He opened the door and said over his shoulder, 'You should derive considerable enjoyment from telling Kelvin that you have a date. Oh, by the way—don't worry about your car. I've rung the garage and arranged for it to be brought in.'

Chapter Two

It was late in the afternoon when Martine came across Sophia and Kelvin, strolling together in the grounds of Sophia's house. Martine had been restless all day, unable to think clearly, unable to erase the face of Loukas Leoros from her mind. She felt afraid, filled as she was with the alarming awareness of the power he was able to exert so easily over her, a power which attacked the mainspring of her defences, leaving her vulnerable and helpless. Yes, he could easily have taken her this morning. Never would she have thought she could be so near surrender and emerge unscathed. What was it about him? She had no need to ask herself that. He was something very special, a man superlative among men, strong and vital. A man to be both respected and feared. A man one would trifle with at one's peril. No use denying that she was drawn to him, that his magnetism was so strong she had to obey its command. Kelvin seemed to be weak in comparison, a spineless creature with numerous flaws in his character.

And here he was, walking with the girl who had taken Martine's place in his affections, the girl responsible for his asking Martine to return his ring.

'Hello, Martine!' Sophia's greeting was cheery and cordial. Martine's teeth clenched together but she managed to say, coolly and with a smile, albeit a forced one, 'Hello, Sophia. Enjoying your walk?'

'Of course.' She snuggled close to Kelvin, who began to look faintly uncomfortable. 'Did Kelvin tell you I was going to Athens with him? We're going tomorrow, for two days.'

'And does your father approve?'

'Papa isn't at home.'

'So he won't know about your trip to Athens?' Martine's glance was for Kelvin. He coloured and made no comment. 'I do not think your father would approve, Sophia,' continued Martine. 'In Greece a young girl does not go off for two days with a man unless he's her husband or some other relative.'

'I don't need you to tell me that,' returned the Greek girl saucily. 'I'm modern! I have been to school in Athens and all of us there have decided we shall not be victims of ancient and out-dated customs. If Papa doesn't approve then I shall leave home!' The girl's dark impressive eyes lifted provocatively to the man at her side, holding his gaze as she added, 'We shall be married, won't we, Kelvin?'

'Not yet awhile,' he said, appearing rather more uncomfortable now.

'I'd like to talk to you, Kelvin. It's about us—and my job,' Martine interrupted.

'I hope you won't leave me until I can find someone else,' he said anxiously. Somehow, his whole manner seemed contemptuous.

'You're asking the impossible.' She thought of last night, and her misery and fear on that lonely road. Kelvin had not bothered to come after her. She might have had an accident for all he cared. The quarrel had been swift, its culmination the return of the ring. And then she had said she was going to Athens, and would then travel back to England. She had taken one suitcase, aware that it was mainly for effect because she felt sure Kelvin would come after her and everything would be all right. There would be a wonderful making up. Well, it was not Kelvin who had rescued her, but another man, a man whom she could not put from her mind no matter how hard she tried.

'I cannot manage without a secretary,' he protested.

'Last night I was going away. You'd have had to manage without a secretary.'

'I knew you'd not go far. You've more common-sense than to run off leaving most of your belongings behind. I waited up for awhile but then went to bed knowing you'd be here this morning.'

'My car isn't here.' She looked squarely at him. 'How do you suppose I managed to get back without my car?'

He shot her a glance of surprise. 'I didn't know your car wasn't here, Martine.'

She remembered that she had mentioned her intention to put the car in the garage instead of leaving it out as she had always done. 'Well, it isn't here. It broke down on the road.'

'It did?' The concern came through, but not very strongly. 'I'd have come out had I known.'

Her mouth curved scornfully. 'You couldn't know anything unless you did come to look for me, could you?'

He went red and she found herself comparing him with Loukas. 'I would certainly have been worried if I had known—'

'Shall we change the subject, Kelvin?' broke in Martine gently. 'It's becoming absurd, don't you think?'

His colour deepened. Sophia, aware of his discomfiture, pulled at the arm she held and urged him to continue their stroll. 'It'll be getting dark,' she added, looking with annoyance at Martine. 'If you want to talk to Kelvin then do it later. I'm sure there isn't anything urgent, and we were so much enjoying our walk.'

'You won't leave me?' said Kelvin as he was being pulled away.

'I have already left you—'

"But—'

'You see, I am getting married very soon and my husband won't want me to continue working for a man to whom I was once engaged.'

'You're getting married!' from Sophia incredulously. As for Kelvin, he just stared at her in total disbelief.

'Yes, Sophia, getting married.' What had she said? How was she to extricate herself from this position she had stupidly managed to get herself into? Martine cursed herself for her impetuosity, her craving for retaliation.

'But you don't know anyone!' Sophia looked almost crestfallen. It suddenly struck Martine that a large part of what she felt for Kelvin was the result of satisfaction at having stolen him from another girl. There was nothing deep between them, and Martine, watching Sophia's expression, rather thought that it was very possible that Kelvin himself might be thrown over before very long.

'You're not serious,' he said with conviction.

'I'd scarcely say I was getting married unless it was true.'

He shook his head from side to side, slowly, as if endeavouring to gather his thoughts. 'Who is the man—No, there isn't any man! You *are* joking—being nasty to get your own back!'

'Have it how you will,' shrugged Martine. She turned and began to walk away. Kelvin came after her, gripping her arm and forcing her to face him.

'Is this true?' he demanded looking grey about the mouth.

'I shan't waste time trying to convince you, Kelvin,' she said, wrenching herself from his hold. 'I'll invite you to the wedding instead.' And on that parting shot she hurried away, not stopping until she had entered her apartment. Then putting her head in her hands she wept bitterly.

Contrary to her expectations, the evening out with Loukas was most enjoyable. He was a charming companion, attentive in every way, his whole attitude a revelation to Martine who, with no experience of men other than Kelvin, now realised that the man she loved possessed the kind of disposition that left a lot to be desired. Loukas took her to a restaurant some distance from Olympia, a superb place elegantly equipped, where the food was as exceptional as the white-coated waiters who served it. Loukas was known there, and treated with both cordiality and deference.

He suggested they sit in the lounge first, where they could have an aperitif and look at the menu. A *bouzouki* band was playing and there were flowers everywhere. It was a lovely, intimate setting and Martine wondered why Kelvin had never brought her here.

'You are not drinking, Martine.' Loukas's voice came to her and she managed a smile.

'I was thinking,' she said.

'About my suggestion?'

'About Kelvin. I was wondering why he never brought me here. It's a most attractive place.'

'I like it.'

'You've brought many women here?'

Faintly he smiled and for a space he seemed far away. 'Only one,' he answered at length. 'Besides you, that is.'

One other. . . .

'Have you never been in love?' she heard herself asking on impulse.

'I believe I have already told you my views on love.'

'That isn't an answer to my question.'

Leaning forward, Loukas picked up the menu left by the waiter. 'Choose what you are having to eat,' he urged and she coloured, aware she had been snubbed.

However, the meal was a huge success, with Loukas chatting to her, sending her admiring glances, flattering her and laughing if she showed the slightest sign of embarrassment.

'My friends call me Luke,' he told her eventually. 'I shall expect my wife to do the same.'

'Your wife?' with assumed surprise.

'You,' briefly, and with a look of censure at her play-acting.

'I can't—'

'I believe you have already made up your mind,' he broke in softly. 'You see, Sophia was speaking to me just before I called for you. She came up to my house to see one of my servants who is rather good at sewing. Sophia wanted her to make a dress for her. Sophia asked me if I knew whom you were marrying. She seemed rather angry that you had found yourself another fiancé so soon after she had been clever enough to entice your first one away.'

'Sophia is a—!' Martine pulled herself up hastily.

Luke glanced at her with perception and said, in some amusement, 'A cat. Yes, you are quite right, that's exactly what she is.'

'I ought not to think rotten things about her. It's not her fault; she's no more than a child.'

'Sophia's nineteen—'

'Nineteen! But she looks only seventeen.'

'And acts like fifteen. How old are you, Martine?'

'Twenty-three.'

'Seven years younger than I. It's sufficient. I'd not want it to be more.'

'I haven't said I'll marry you,' she began when Luke silenced her with an imperative flip of his fingers.

'Drink your wine,' he urged.

'So you are thirty. I had guessed correctly.'

'You were interested enough to take a guess at my age?'

'It was automatic.'

He laughed and she caught her breath. The scar was scarcely visible, so everything about him was handsome. She had previously noted his clothes—the white linen suit, the shirt of pale mauve, fashionably frilled; she had noted too the gleaming hair brushed back as if he would curb the waves, the faint yet pervasive odour of his after-shave lotion. She wondered if he had noticed her perfume. . . . But what did she care if he had or not?

'I must tell you about myself,' she heard him saying as she lifted her glass in obedience to his order. 'I'm in shipping mainly—running cruise ships in the Mediterranean and sometimes in the Caribbean. I also have two hotels in Athens and one on the island of Skiathos. I must take you there soon. You'll like it. But first of all I want you to see Mykonos.'

'You're taking far too much for granted.'

'I have spoken with Sophia, remember. Or, rather, she has spoken with me.'

'What answer did you give her when she asked whom I was—er—supposed to be marrying?'

'I said she would hear soon enough. I also assured her that it was no rumour; you were definitely getting married.'

'It seems strange that she should ask you.'

'I have known Sophia since she was twelve.'

'But she didn't know that you were acquainted with me.'

'She knew that I'd have heard the gossip.'

'Gossip?'

'Your forthcoming marriage.'

'Only yesterday I was engaged to Kelvin.'

'Then people will say you're a fast worker,' he returned in a voice which held a mingling of mockery and humour.

'There hasn't been any gossip,' she said, replacing her glass on the table. 'Sophia learned about my marriage—you know what I mean—from me. I never mentioned your name so what made her ask you whom I was marrying?'

'She didn't ask it outright,' he admitted after a pause. 'She merely said that the girl who had been engaged to Kelvin Gresham had said she was getting married to someone else. Sophia's curiosity was well and truly aroused and she asked me if I knew anything about it.'

'Sophia has a sister,' mentioned Martine, and then wondered why, for it was totally irrelevant. But her eyes widened when she looked up from her plate and saw the harsh expression on her companion's face. His lips were compressed; his eyes glittered and his nostrils seemed to flare. 'Is—is something the matter?' she asked, her knife and fork idle in her hands.

'Nothing,' he said curtly and then with an abrupt change of subject, 'You haven't yet told me about yourself. Have you parents—brothers and sisters?'

'My parents died within six months of each other when I was twenty. I sold the house and bought a flat close to where I was working, as secretary to the Managing Director of a paint firm. At week-ends I used to help at an archaeological site and that was where I met Kelvin.'

'Love at first sight, I suppose,' remarked Luke cynically.

'He asked me to be his secretary.'

'And you left an excellent post to accept his offer? It must have been love at first sight.'

'According to you there is no such thing as love.'

'But according to you there is—and it's you we're talking about.'

'I must admit he attracted me.'

'But not in the same way that I attract you?'

She had to laugh at his audacity. 'You don't happen to attract me at all,' she began.

'Liar,' softly and admonishingly. 'You and I attract one another; we cannot do without each other, Martine, and the sooner you are as honest as I the happier you will be.'

'I'd never be happy without love in my marriage.'

An impatient breath escaped him. 'Even if there was such a thing as love it's so fragile that it's doomed from the start.'

'What a cynic you are!'

'I'm practical, not prone to living in the clouds and looking down at life through rose-coloured spectacles. Be realistic, child, and see things as they really are, not as you would like them to be.'

'I want romance,' she said wistfully. 'You wouldn't understand.'

'Romance!' he scoffed, beckoning the waiter to have him top up their glasses. 'Be satisfied with physical enjoyment,' he advised. 'It is tangible; this thing called romance is not.'

'Because you haven't experienced it—' Martine broke off, not at all sure that he had never known what romance was.

'It's time we changed the subject,' decided Luke. 'We must fix a date for our wedding.'

She frowned at him across the table, trying to look severe and aloof when in reality she felt trapped . . . and very young and helpless. Somehow she was being driven along a path she had no wish to take and she was shocked to realise that resignation was gradually creeping into her consciousness. But surely she could fight! There was no one on earth who could force her into a marriage unless she really wanted it.

'I'm not marrying you!' Determination in her tone and a glitter of resolution in her eyes.

Luke said quietly, 'There's no need for such vehemence. We shall talk outside, when we've finished our meal.'

An hour later they were walking in the moonlit gardens of the restaurant. 'There's a seat over there,' said Luke pointing. 'Among the trees.'

Where he had taken the 'other one,' she decided, unwilling to visualise him sitting there with someone else. She put the matter from her and said, as he took her hand, 'You'll not persuade me, Luke.'

'On Friday we shall go to Athens for the engagement and wedding rings. We'll stay the night in a cosy little hotel I know of.'

'I wish you'd listen to me!'

'Martine,' he said softly, 'do not keep up this absurd attitude; it annoys me.'

'But—'

'Be quiet!' he commanded and she found herself obeying despite the urge to throw him a tart rejoinder and then turn on her heel and run.

They sat down; Martine stared at the sky through the spidery foliage of the tall palms, watching the clouds unfold so that the moon could emerge again after it had disappeared for a space. Stars came out, too, millions of them spangling the heavens. Restless, she stood up and moved away from Luke. What did she want? She knew without any doubt at all that, should he decide to leave her, to say good night and go, she would want to sit down and cry.

She was conscious of him behind her, felt his fingers cobweb light and tantalising on her neck; they moved to her ears and a quiver passed through her, a feeling of rapt, all-pervading ecstasy. His hands moved again and now it was her shoulders they were caressing, and the insides of her arms. She tried to fight off the natural reaction to the temptation, tried to remain immune, but he was too clever, for her or any other woman; he had had too much practice for him to fail, she decided, as a kind of delicious invigoration swept like an avalanche over her body. She turned without being coerced, turned willingly in exquisite eagerness, vitally aware of him as a man, aware that he was communicating his passion to her, his fierce pagan ardour as, sweeping her into his arms, he rained kisses on her mouth and throat, the tender soft valley between her breasts. She tried to murmur a protest but refrained, admitting it would not only be insincere but also futile. His hands strayed, one cupping her breast while the other slid down to her waist and further, possessively, arrogantly, as if his explorations were a challenge that she might or might not care to accept. She smiled a knowing smile and decided to resist, just a little. She caught his hand, said a firm 'no' and found her own hands imprisoned and held behind her back.

'Fight me if you want,' he said mockingly, 'but I shall always win.'

'You have an inflated opinion of yourself!'

'I understand women. All females, whatever the species, are susceptible to male dominance. He drew her to him again, this time making sure her arms were imprisoned at her sides. She was soon lost once more in the whirlpool of his passion; she joined him in the rhythmic swaying of his body, pressed herself in rapturous seeking against his masculine strength. She, too, became primitive, fierce in her desire to be fulfilled.

He said raggedly against her breast, 'You'll marry me? Say it, because if you don't you know full well you'll become my pillow friend.'

'And that is not really what you want.' A statement, and he made no response. And after awhile, as his hands and eager mouth began to roam again, she heard herself say in husky, whispered tones, 'Yes, Luke, I will marry you—just as soon as you want me to.'

Martine sat on a fallen column and stared fixedly at the magnificent spectacle of the Parthenon, its weathered, ochre-tinted stonework mellowed by time and the elements of nature. She tried to imagine what it had been like when it stood in its pristine beauty—when its columns were glistening white, for they were made of Pentellic marble, used by the builders of the age.

She glanced up as Luke's tall, distinguished figure came into view. He had told her to wait here for an hour as he had some business to do—this after they had visited the jewellers in the city and she had chosen the rings, chosen them almost against her will because so many doubts were running riot in her mind. That she was being coerced and used was evident, and yet she seemed to have no will to fight the wave of Luke's dominance. Will . . . ? She felt that perhaps it had nothing to do with willpower after all; desire was her paramount emotion . . . and she knew she desired Luke as a lover. Shame gave way to a sort of defiance as she thought of what was natural to males and females of every species . . . mating.

'A drachma for your thoughts, Martine.' The

voice, so attractive with its alien accent, the half smile that was yet undisguisedly mocking, the enigmatic expression in those black eyes. . . . Was it any wonder she was attracted to such a man? Tall and straight, his shoulders broad, his very stance gave the impression of superiority and she felt that had he lived in those ancient times of tribal warfare in Greece he would have been a king.

'I cannot tell you what I was thinking,' she replied, picking up the drachma he had dropped into her lap. 'So I will return your money.' She held it up. His hand enclosed hers and she was brought to her feet. 'The people,' she began, glancing around at the numbers of tourists surrounding tired and hoarse guides, cameras at the ready. 'You can't. . . .' She trailed off to silence as he laughed.

'Why do you always assume that I want to kiss you?' he asked, looking down at her in some amusement.

'You said we were going to have lunch in the Plaka,' she said, averting her eyes. 'It's half past one.'

'Changing the subject, eh?' He tucked her arm in his. 'I think this occasion calls for something special. We shall lunch at the Grande Bretagne.'

It was Athens' most elegant hotel and Martine felt pleased that Luke should decide to take her there on this special occasion.

After lunch they went up on the roof, and there, with the spectacular view of the city spread before them, with the heights of Lycabettus shining in the sun, Luke took her hand and slid the diamond and emerald ring on to her finger. She stared at it, fascinated by the dark clarity of the stones, her mind in a daze and her sensations muddled. For while on the one hand she accepted that all this was madness, on the other hand she had the strange conviction that Fate dominated the situation, that on the day she was born it had been laid down that she should marry this tall, handsome Greek, be his wife and lover for as long as Fate decreed.

'It's beautiful,' she breathed, passing a finger across the ring. Luke tilted her face with an imperious finger beneath her chin, bent his head and kissed her parted lips.

'You chose it,' he reminded her a moment later. 'You have excellent taste.'

She smiled faintly. It was easy to have good taste when the cost did not come into it.

'Have what you really like,' Luke had said. 'You have to live with it for the rest of your life.'

'Let us have a bottle of champagne in the lounge,' he suggested and she felt that, for once in his life, he was acting solely on impulse.

'I feel I have had enough wine already,' she demurred.

'Nonsense. Come, let us go down . . . and celebrate.'

Why the hesitation? she wondered, then thought that perhaps there had been no hesitation, that she had only imagined it.

The champagne was brought to them as they sat in a corner of the lounge; the bottle was half empty when, having picked it up to refill their glasses, Luke's attention became fixed and his whole expression changed so dramatically that Martine felt her heart give a little lurch. His face looked almost evil, the features twisted, the nostrils flaring. And then, just as dramatically, his face resumed its former serenity as a smile came to his lips. He put the bottle down and rose to his feet. Following the direction of his gaze Martine saw a tall, incredibly beautiful and sophisticated girl coming towards their table, a Greek girl whose poise was almost intimidating, whose air of self-confidence made Martine feel like a child just out of school.

'Odette,' softly and with a deepening of his smile. 'I thought you were travelling in Europe to recover from your traumatic experience.'

Martine's eyes darted to his. The subtle, undercurrent of sarcasm, of contempt. . . . Surely the girl must have recognised it! If so, she chose to assume a pose of affable ignorance as she stretched out her hand to place it in the lean brown one extended to her while her alert dark eyes slid with swift appraisal to Martine, sitting there and feeling totally out of place.

'Divorce is no longer a traumatic experience,' she said with a light laugh that reminded Martine of the tinkle of sheep bells in a meadow. 'It was so simple, Luke; you have no idea!'

Her glance slid again to Martine and Luke said, his tone void of expression, 'Odette, meet Martine, my fiancée. Martine—Odette Manolis —daughter of your landlord, Mr. Sotiris.'

'How do you do?' Martine automatically held out her hand.

'Your . . . finacée?' Odette's lovely eyes were wide and disbelieving. 'You—you can't be serious. Why, all these years you have never—' She shook her head, mumbling something in her own tongue. Luke stopped her with an arrogant flick of a finger. It was plain that he had no intention of allowing the girl to talk in Greek.

'Martine and I became engaged an hour or so ago.' He paused a moment and then, with slow deliberation that was in the nature of a challenge, 'Aren't you going to congratulate us? Wish us well?'

Looking at her, Martine shivered at the coldly venomous glitter in the Greek girl's eyes. It seemed an eternity before Odette said, her brittle smile as forced as the words that left her lips, 'Of course. Congratulations, Loukas.' She turned to Martine. 'And to you . . . much happiness.'

Martine went cold. This, she knew without any doubt at all, was the girl whom Luke had once loved. Yes, despite his views on love, his flat denial of its existence, he had once been in love.

And the girl he had loved had married someone else. She was now free and Luke, fearing he would fall victim to her charms again, had also decided to marry someone else.

Chapter Three

As soon as Odette left them Martine turned to Luke. 'You were once in love with her.' It was a statement, calmly spoken and just as calmly received.

'It was inevitable that you would guess that there had been something between Odette and me.'

'You were in love with her,' persisted Martine.

'There was no love on her side.' Luke took up the champagne bottle and seemed to become absorbed in a study of the label.

'I was talking about you, Luke,' said Martine, still persistent. 'You said you did not believe in love between a man and a woman, and I suspected your words were due to disillusionment. You *did* love Odette, and she let you down.'

Silence, while Luke poured the wine. 'As you have guessed so much I will tell you the rest,' he then said, surprising her, for she had half suspected he would tell her to mind her own business. 'Odette and I were betrothed; whatever I felt for her was deep—but I was young,' he added swiftly, as if by way of an excuse for some incredible folly. 'I was twenty-three and she a year younger. She swore she loved me and, I must confess, we had wonderful times together. My father was living, and an elder brother who was his sole heir. In Greece a younger son does not expect to inherit much,' he explained. 'And so Odette began to cool off when someone else came along, a wealthy hotelier whose flattery— and fortune—went to her head.' Luke paused, and again Martine saw that harsh and evil expression mar his features. 'She married him—' He broke off abruptly and now there was both pain and bitterness on his face. It was plain that he had suffered by the girl's action in throwing him over. 'As you heard, she is now divorced.'

'And free,' inserted Martine, watching his expression closely. It was a mask, unreadable. 'She was obviously taken aback to hear you were engaged.'

Luke picked up his glass and, for a long moment, sat staring at the bubbles coming to the top. 'She wrote to me recently to ask if we could take up where we left off.'

'And you are afraid—'

'Of what?' harshly, and with a glitter in his eye.

'Of falling for her again, which means that you *do* believe in love.' Martine waited, her nerves tensed. Until this moment she had been undecided about marrying him, had known that it was not too late to change her mind. Yes, she realised, that had been at the back of her consciousness even while she was allowing herself to be driven by Luke's dominance and her own physical desire. But now she knew that she really wanted to marry Luke, that within her there was an unfathomable emotion and a need that had nothing to do with sex or the pleasure she would derive from it as Luke's lover. 'You do believe in love,' repeated Martine, determined to have a straight answer from him.

He looked at her, his expression still inscrutable. 'I do not believe in love between a man and a woman,' he said at last.

'But you loved Odette?'

'I was infatuated with her.'

Martine drew an impatient breath and suddenly her companion laughed.

'Forget it,' he advised. 'I learned a lesson— which is never to feel too deeply about a woman.'

She frowned, vitally aware of that sensation within her that was a world apart from anything physical. She did not try to analyse it, nor even to examine it too closely. It was there; it might stay or it might go. Time alone would tell.

'Your brother died, I take it?'

He nodded, putting his glass to his lips. 'Soon after Odette . . . jilted me. Father died less than a year later.'

'So you became wealthy after all.' There was a quality of genuine indifference in her tone which told him that, to her, his fortune and what it would provide were immaterial.

'I inherited everything, yes.' Luke's voice was brusque now, as if he felt he had confided quite enough and would deter her from asking any more questions.

She picked up her glass and drank deeply,

then wanted to sneeze. She controlled the impulse and said lightly, 'If I drink any more you will have to carry me out of here.'

'A pleasure.' All seriousness was gone; they went from the hotel into the sunshine and bustle of Athens, Martine's hand in his. She was happy at this moment; the future could take care of itself.

'Can I have a proper wedding dress?' she asked and her fiancé lifted his brows a fraction.

'What do you mean by that? Certainly you shall have a proper wedding dress.'

'I thought perhaps you wanted it to be very quiet.'

'Not at all. We shall have a wedding to remember.'

'Even though it is based on spite—revenge—' She broke off, but too late. 'I didn't mean to say anything like that,' she murmured, biting her lip.

'Spite and revenge. . . .' He was thoughtful as they walked along, then stopped among the vast crowd waiting to cross the road. 'Not much on which to base a successful marriage, you are thinking? Well, my dear, it is not only that. It is mainly the physical attraction we have for one another that will make our union successful.'

She made no comment, for what he said was true. They were both depending on the sexual draw . . . and if ever that should fail . . . ?

That evening they dined at the hotel in a romantic setting of candlelight and music and soft-footed waiters. They ate Greek food and drank champagne again and afterwards they went into the city and up to the Acropolis to witness the famous 'sound and light' spectacular. All was magic—the illuminated temples, so ancient and evocative, the voices, strong and imperious. It was all new and exciting for Martine, who was able to forget all about Kelvin and his inconstancy. But she was no fool; she knew she would feel again the deep hurt, knew that this was merely an interval of forgetfulness that would disappear and leave her thinking again of her broken engagement, and of what might have been if Sophia had not come upon the scene.

'It seems strange that both your hurt and mine were caused by two sisters,' she murmured, voicing what had been in her mind since she had been introduced to Odette and discovered what she had meant to Luke.

'Ironic,' he agreed. 'But it was meant to be. I believe in Fate.'

'So do I. Our lives are mapped out when we are born.'

He looked at her, his face in the bright light more handsome and severe than ever, with the scar scarcely noticeable.

'So you admit that you were meant to marry me?'

She heaved a sigh and said, 'I suppose so.'

'Then stop worrying about Kelvin and your broken engagement.'

'I'm not worrying.'

'Perhaps not consciously at this moment because other things are here to occupy your mind —you're excited, for one thing. But tomorrow when we arrive home you'll have time to think, and brood. Don't even think of changing your mind, though,' he warned with a stern inflection, 'because if you do you'll regret it.'

She had no intention of changing her mind but she was curious and so impelled to say, 'In what way shall I regret it?'

"I mean to have you.'

'Yes?' with a frown of bewilderment.

'And if it's not to be marriage then you shall be my pillow friend.'

Her frown deepened. 'You could never force me to be that,' she asserted with conviction.

'My dear Martine,' he said with a hint of asperity, 'you are as putty in my hands. The repeated betrayal of your emotions is probably more transparent than you imagine. I could take you whenever I liked . . . and having slept with me once you could not resist sleeping with me again, and again. . . .'

Martine snatched her hand from his. 'I hate you when you talk like that!'

'But not enough to throw me over.' The statement angered her but she made no comment for all that. Luke spoke again to remind her that it was not as a pillow friend he wanted her and, should he be forced to take her as that, it would obviously be only the prelude to marriage. 'Because you are the kind of girl who would prefer marriage to the other,' he added finally.

'You appear to understand me perfectly,' she said through lips that had gone dry and stiff.

'Let us change the subject,' he urged. 'Or, better still, let us concentrate on the performance.'

Later, when they had had a bite of supper in the hotel lounge, with quiet *bouzouki* music drifting through the elegant room, Luke escorted Martine to her room and before she had time to utter the swift 'good night' she had intended and close the door on him he was inside the room and it was he who was closing the door. She moved quickly towards the window, ostensibly to draw the drapes. But the window was open and she would have to close it first.

Luke came to her, drew her away and towards him. His mouth found hers, hot and sensuously exploring, compelling her to part her lips so his tongue could find the sweet dark hollows, caress in rough possession. His hands were equally exploring, one sliding from her slender waist to move across her stomach while the other closed on her breast, the long, lean fingers possessing the nipple, closing tightly on it, while all the time he was pressing her body against his, demanding that she know and understand the strength of his passion. She felt his hand move from her breast to caress her most sensitive places, his fingers expertly gentle, feather-soft on her throat, her ear, her temple where the blue veins tinted the delicate alabaster of her skin.

Martine arched her soft young body in a kind of supplication when, her own desires ignited by the burning fires of his, she abandoned all resistance and gave herself up to the exquisite joy of surrender. Eventually he held her at arms' length so that he could devour her beauty, look deeply into eyes dark and torpid with passion about to flare.

Softly he laughed, the laugh of the victor, and he picked her up, walking rhythmically towards the bed. Only then did she begin to struggle, and because it was his will and not hers that he should release her, she was set down on her feet. Luke bent and kissed her, gently, as his fingers traced a line from the delicate curve of her throat where a pulse throbbed uncontrollably to the tender lobe of her breast where they rested, teasingly, until she uttered a little moan and twisted away, her cheeks burning, her whole body on fire, heated to torment by the stimulation of his lips and his hands and the virile hardness of his frame.

'Please go,' she mumbled in a voice she scarcely recognised as her own. 'It isn't right for you to be here.'

A smile of mocking amusement curved his chiselled mouth. 'On the contrary, it is very right. I ought to stay,' he continued, his perceptive eyes intently scrutinising her face. 'You're in the mood and so am I. It's not natural for us to desist now.'

'You sound clinical and I dislike your manner intensely!'

'Are you trying to find something more here than sex?' he inquired and a frown touched his forehead as he spoke.

'Of course not!'

But was she? The idea had not occurred to her until this moment when he had mentioned it. Did she want more than he could give? Something spiritual, for instance? But that would entail love, which neither could give the other— she because of her love for Kelvin, and he because of the disillusionment he had suffered at the hands of Odette.

'Then don't,' was Luke's advice as he turned towards the door. 'Never ask for too much from life.' He paused on the threshold. 'I'm leaving even through I know I ought to stay.' The fine lips curved in a smile that was both cynical and mocking. 'It's no consolation to me to know that once I'm through that door you'll regret asking me to leave.'

Martine's teeth snapped together. 'Your arrogance and pomposity stick in my gullet!' she threw at him furiously. 'Be careful, or I might change my mind!'

To that he made no response, but merely smiled a knowing smile and left the room, quietly closing the door behind him.

Martine had not been home an hour when Kelvin knocked on her door and entered the living-room at her invitation. She looked at him in surprise as it suddenly occurred to her that he was supposed to be in Athens. He had changed his mind about going, he said tersely.

'You've come to talk about my job,' she said coldly. 'I didn't consider it necessary, under the circumstances, to give you the customary notice. I have left your employ, as I said, so there isn't anything we have to talk about.'

'Yes, there is,' he said grimly and with a glowering look. 'This thing about your getting married. I've thought about it and I can't accept it—'

'There isn't any reason why you should, or why you should not,' she broke in, marvelling at the calm manner she was able to adopt. 'When you broke our engagement your interest in my life ceased.'

He stood with his back to the window, studying her intently. 'I can't quite make you out.' It was a complaint, spoken like a child in a fractious mood, and suddenly Martine wondered how she had ever come to look up to him as she had. True, his appearance was something special, and she had been interested in his work, which had been an added incentive for her to admire him. But when she compared him with Luke . . . 'You're not really getting married, are you?'

For answer she held out her hand. 'An engagement ring,' she supplied, when it seemed he was too dumbfounded to utter even one word.

'But who—?' He shook his head, gritting his teeth. 'You don't know anybody round here!'

'I know Luke Leoros,' she corrected quietly. 'It is he whom I'm marrying. He lives in the large white villa on the hill.'

Kelvin stared in astounded disbelief. 'It's not true!' And then, inconsistently, 'You must have been carrying on with him while you were engaged to me!'

'Then that made two of us. You were carrying on with Sophia.'

He took a threatening step towards her, then stopped, his whole manner undergoing a change. 'You're doing this for revenge,' he accused and now his voice was quiet and faintly concerned. 'There's obviously much I don't understand, but if this is true, Martine, then you must be out of your mind. The shock of our broken engagement's affected you far more than I had anticipated. After all, engagements are broken all the time, and it's my opinion that it is far better to realise one's mistake before marriage than after—at least it's simpler to put right.'

'You're so casual about it,' she returned bitterly. 'To me, our engagement was permanent; it meant what it was intended to mean— a pact, an act of faith—' She broke off and shrugged her shoulders. 'What is the use of all this talking? You and I are through, so much so that you are marrying someone else and so am I. If there's nothing else you want to say then please go. I have things to do.'

'You're making a big mistake in marrying on the rebound like this, Martine. For heaven's sake, let me help you. There must be something I can do.'

Martine's smile was bitter. 'Do you really believe that?'

He studied her face, noticing the pallor that had come to it while they had been talking. Her mouth was moving convulsively and her eyes were darkly shadowed.

'I feel a cad,' he admitted unexpectedly. 'I don't know if I'm doing the right thing in letting you go. Sophia's young, immature. . . .' His voice trailed into silence with a deep and heavy intake of breath. 'Perhaps you and I ought to think again. . . .' Again his voice petered out as he saw her shake her head.

'I'm engaged to Luke,' she said quietly. 'He'd never release me even if I wanted him to.'

'Never release you?' Angrily and with a frown. 'He could do nothing if you were to decide to give him his ring back.'

'Obviously you don't know him very well,' was Martine's dry rejoinder.

'Are you telling me he would threaten you?'

'I'm not telling you anything, since it's occurred to me that a man like you would never understand a man like Luke. You're weak in comparison, Kelvin, though I am sorry to say it.'

'Weak!' he flashed, dark colour creeping up the sides of his mouth. 'That's an insult, Martine!'

'Sorry, but I have spoken only the truth.' She glanced at her watch. 'I must ask you to leave. I'm going to Luke's for dinner and he told me to be there at seven o'clock.'

'You're out of your mind! Mad!'

'I don't agree, but even if I were out of my mind it would not be any of your business.' She preceded him to the door and opened it.

'I've a pile of typing,' he muttered. 'How am I going to get it done?'

'Sophia—'

'Can't type and you know it!'

'Then she can learn. It strikes me that she has lived the idle life far too long. It's time she did something useful for a change.' The last sentence was significant and Kelvin caught on to it at once.

'You're jealous of her!'

'Any engaged girl would be jealous of another who took her fiancé from her,' Martine was honest enough to admit. But she did add, without malice or spite, 'You might come to regret giving me up, Kelvin, for I rather think that Sophia can be fickle.'

'That's nasty!'

'It wasn't meant to be. After all,'' she added after a slight pause, 'you yourself have just said she's young and immature and that you are already beginning to regret—'

'I said no such thing,' interrupted Kelvin hotly.

'You implied it when you said that you and I had better think again—' She stopped, frowning impatiently. 'This is getting us nowhere! I have asked you to go, so please do just that!'

It was twenty minutes to eight when Martine arrived at the magnificent white villa that was soon to be her home. She had on a long dress of pale green organza, low-cut and fitting snugly to her curves. The skirt was full-flowing from a nipped-in waist; the whole design was simple, its attraction in the colour combined with the expert cut. Over it she wore a cape of black velvet and she carried a black velvet evening bag trimmed with tiny silver beads. A last glance in the mirror had more than satisfied her and, as she stood on the top of the flight of white marble steps leading to the front door of the villa, she knew a sense of excitement which totally overshadowed the depression that had settled on her after Kelvin's departure.

'Miss Lawson. Please come in.' The manservant who opened the door smiled as he stood aside for her to enter. 'My master is expecting you. He say for me to show you into the salon and he will be with you in one—two minutes.'

'Thank you.'

'My name is Hermes,' he submitted as he closed the door. 'If you will follow me, please.'

Martine glanced around as she passed through the hall, noting the huge urns of copper and bronze in which palms and poinsettias and many other plants and flowers flourished. A bougainvillaea climbed round an archway, its roots set in a massive pewter vase whose handles were fashioned in a style similar to those of ancient Greek vases that Martine had seen in the Athens Museum. Wealth and good taste characterised everything, both in the hall and in the salon into which she was being shown. She felt awestruck, rather dazed, as she tried to accept that this was to be her home, that she would be the mistress here, with servants, too. Somewhat timidly she moved around the room, fingering Georgian silver candlesticks, Sevrès china and the incomparable Chelsea-Derby group set so delightfully on a Jabobean oak table by the window. The carpet seemed like foam rubber beneath her feet, the drapes were of Italian silk, beautifully embroidered. She lifted her eyes to the ceiling and saw that it had been decorated with gold leaf and distinctive strap-work.

She swung around as the door opened. Luke, superlatively attired in a suit of buff linen with a white shirt beneath the loose-fitting jacket, stood for a long moment, his appraising eyes travelling over his visitor from her gleaming head to her dainty toes peeping from the silver kid sandals she was wearing. She coloured adorably, and passed her tongue over her lips that had quite suddenly gone dry. She felt embarrassed, ill-at-ease, inadequate. But Luke came forward as if aware of how she was feeling, his hands outstretched. She shyly put hers into them, noticing his swift glance at her ring. She was drawn close; she felt the warm gentleness of his hand as he tilted her chin so that he could look into her eyes.

'You're more lovely than ever,' he murmured, taking her cape from her shoulders and dropping it on to a chair. Then he kissed her, his hand sliding into her hair, curling round it, bringing golden strands to his face. She was vitally aware of his attractiveness, aware that a thousand women would love to be where she was at this moment. How had such a man come to choose her for his wife? Despite the fact of his not loving her, it still seemed like a miracle that he had ever even noticed her. His hands cupped her face; she knew the delight of the musky smell of him which seemed to mingle with a pervasive blend of heather and wild thyme—after-shave, no doubt, or maybe an expensive body lotion. Whatever it was it stirred her senses, stimulating the desire for closeness, for the sensitive touch of his hands, the contact of his flesh with hers.

'I—I'm sorry to be late,' she managed at last. 'I was—er—delayed.'

'You took too long in getting ready?' He quirked an eyebrow and added, 'It was worth it so I shall forgive you.'

'Kelvin called,' she told him briefly.

'He did?' Luke's voice was terse. 'And what did he want?'

'He didn't believe I was engaged to be married.'

'That's understandable,' said Luke reasonably. 'After all, it's only four days since you and he parted.'

'He said I was crazy to marry on the rebound.'

'Are you marrying on the rebound?' Luke moved with ease and grace towards a drinks cabinet. Martine thought he glided rather than walked.

'I suppose I must be,' she answered thoughtfully. 'I mean—the speed. . . .'

'I firmly believe that if Kelvin hadn't broken the engagement then you would have. We have already agreed that Fate decreed that you and I would marry. We were destined to meet the way we did.'

'You would have—tempted me, while I was still engaged to Kelvin?' Martine moved towards a couch and sat down.

'Of course, when I realised I wanted you.'

'I might have remained loyal to Kelvin. After all, I loved him.'

'You'd have come to me,' he said confidently.

'As for loving him—' He broke off and turned and she saw the sardonic humour in his eyes. 'Who are you trying to convince—yourself or me?'

'I still love him.'

'What would you like to drink?'

'I *do* love him! What kind of a woman would I be if I could fall out of love so easily?'

'Ah, I see now what is troubling you. You've a guilt complex because you're not sitting at home weeping copious tears and telling yourself that your life is finished, that all you can see ahead is a long dark road with a lonely death at the end of it.' A laugh escaped him, a cynical laugh, harsh-edged and acting like a rasp on Martine's ear-drums. 'You're young; your hurt's already begun to heal, and soon you'll be agreeing with me that there is no such thing as love between a man and a woman. You, my child, were no more in love than I was.'

'With Odette?' she asked, for the moment diverted from her own situation.

'As I said, it was nothing stronger than infatuation.'

But was it? Martine felt that Luke was glossing over it far too lightly, that he was adopting a cold resolve never to admit, even to himself, that he had ever been in love. He had been hurt, badly, and how could that be unless he had loved Odette? Loved her deeply and sincerely?

Without warning a heavy weight settled on Martine's heart. She did not want to know that Luke had been in love with another girl . . . and yet she did know, and she felt that nothing could ever erase the knowledge from her mind.

Luke was speaking again, asking her what she would like to drink.

'A dry martini, please.'

'On the rocks?'

She nodded her head. 'And with a dash of lemon, please.'

He smiled, poured it and brought it to her, standing for a moment above her, toweringly tall; his dark eyes settled on the glass in his hand as he moved it to hear the ice tinkle against the sides.

'There will be no dark road for you, Martine,' he said at last. 'You'll have children to care for, to take away any loneliness you might at this time envision.' He placed the glass on a small table close to her chair and turned away to get his own drink.

'Children, born without love between their father and mother,' she heard herself say in a low and husky voice.

'It happens all the time.'

'In Greece, yes.'

'Everywhere.'

'You will love your children?'

He turned, a bottle poised over a glass. 'Is that a challenge?' His fine mouth quirked. 'That, my dear, is paternal love and bears no relation to the love you insist can endure between a man and a woman.'

She merely sighed and sipped her drink. It was enough that she was to have him for a husband; she would not ask for more. Did she want more? The idea startled her and she shot him a glance, looking at his features as if seeing them in a different light. Love. . . . No, why should she want his love? She herself had none to give so she could hardly expect love from her husband.

Dinner was in the elegant dining-room, in a setting of candleglow and antique china and cutlery. Music invaded the room from two speakers hidden somewhere in the wide pelmets.

'Shall I ever get used to all this?' Martine spoke softly, almost to herself. 'I feel I'm dreaming and shall waken to reality before very long.'

'This is reality, my dear.' His black eyes roved over her and she felt she was being stripped. 'Not quite,' he amended, eyes glimmering at her disconcerted manner. 'Reality will begin with our marriage.'

With the first night, she thought, trying to imagine what it would be like to sleep with Luke. 'Kelvin says I'm mad, and he could be right.'

'Shall we leave Kelvin out of this? He's nothing to you now and I shall be glad when he's finished his book and taken himself off, back to his own country.'

'The book isn't half done yet, and he's without a secretary.'

'There are secretaries to be had if he looks around.' Luke eased back so that Hermes could serve him the main course.

'I suggested he get Sophia to do some typing for him.'

A low laugh escaped her finacé. 'The mere suggestion that she should do a spot of work would be enough to make her throw him over.'

'You appear to know the girl well.'

'As I said, I've known her since she was twelve. Her parents came here seven years ago, having bought the house about a year previously.' He stopped and became thoughtful; Martine wondered if he were thinking of Odette and realised he must have begun keeping company with her almost as soon as she and her family arrived in Olympia.

Luke changed the subject, saying they must talk about the wedding and fix a date. Martine nodded, feeling excited in spite of the fact that she was entering into a loveless marriage. Luke told her of a dressmaker who would make her a gown that would look as if it had been designed and made in Paris.

'Bridesmaids,' he said. 'You must have someone you can ask?'

'I can only think of Thoula, the girl who comes in to clean for me.'

'She's a charming girl—engaged to Socrates, one of my gardeners. He's waiting for her to provide a dowry and it's taking time because she has only one brother working for it—along with her father, of course.'

'Dowry? She must have a dowry?'

'The custom's dying out in the big towns, but in the small ones it survives, unfortunately. Socrates could marry Thoula if he wished because I've offered him a small villa I own not far from here, but he insists on a dowry, which is a house and land.'

'And Thoula's father and brother have to keep on working until they can buy this house and land?'

'The land's already there, for most peasants own land which they work to make a living. But the house is the burden; building costs are high and materials have to be brought from a distance. Thoula won't be married for several years yet.'

'Can't you persuade Socrates to forego the house?'

'I've tried.' He smiled faintly and said, 'Perhaps you could succeed where I have failed.'

'I shall certainly have a try.' Martine changed

the subject, going back to the question of the bridesmaids. 'I'd like to have two, but I don't know anyone else.'

'I have a cousin. She'll be invited to the wedding so she could be a bridesmaid if you would like.'

'Yes, I would,' eagerly because she was keen to meet a relative of Luke's. She was surprised that he should be showing this much interest; it heartened her, imbuing her with an optimism which had been lacking up till now. 'What's her name?'

'Vasiliki. She's eighteen and betrothed to a boy who's away at London University.'

'It will be nice to meet her,' said Martine enthusiastically.

'I'm sorry I don't have many relatives. My mother died eleven years ago, and I had a sister who died in infancy. However, I do have this cousin, and her parents—my aunt Souphoula and Uncle Demos. You will meet them at the wedding.'

'I'm looking forward to having relatives. I've been on my own so long.'

He nodded thoughtfully. 'That's probably why you became engaged to someone as unsuitable as Kelvin,' he remarked.

He could be right, she thought—then suddenly realised that she was agreeing with him when he said Kelvin was unsuitable.

'We were well-matched!' she shot at him, chin lifting.

He regarded her admonishingly. 'Don't lie, Martine. You know as well as I do that Kelvin is weak, and a weak man is not for you.'

She made no comment, and a short while later

she reluctantly said good night as he stood by her car while she switched on the engine and engaged the gear.

'Tomorrow, then. I'll take you along to see Antiopi, who will be delighted to have the order for your wedding dress.'

Chapter Four

The wedding was over, also the reception. The last of the guests had gone, leaving Martine alone with her husband.

'It's been a wonderful day.' She had to break the silence, a silence that seemed to be stretching to eternity. 'I liked your aunt and uncle. Your aunt's so patient with him. The way he fondles those worry beads would drive me to distraction. Why do so many Greek men twirl those things about all the time?'

Her husband's fine mouth quirked at one corner. He knew she was talking for talking's sake, knew she was uneasy—no, more than that. She was scared.

'Men need the beads to help them forget their worries. Greek women are not supposed to have worries,' he added swiftly, anticipating her question.

'Well, the only worry I have noticed is whether their wives and daughters are working hard enough in the fields!'

A low laugh escaped him. He moved towards her and she stepped back, freeing the delicate lace of her dress, which had become caught on the bold carving of a chair.

'Is this an act or are you genuinely afraid of me?' Luke took another step in her direction.

'All brides are scared.'

Another laugh, cynical this time and filled with mockery as well. 'Then I don't know what of. Few of them are without experience.'

'You seem to know.'

'I know how difficult it is to come by a virgin,' he said and laughed yet again as the colour flooded her face. 'Are you a virgin, Martine?'

She looked straight at him. 'You'd not have married me if you had had any doubts about that.'

'Correct. I hope I didn't make a mistake.'

Her chin lifted. 'You have all the arrogance of a Greek god!' she flashed. 'Perhaps you can tell me how Greek men can expect to marry virgins when they seduce every woman who comes their way?'

'Not every woman, my dear. Some women are respected because they deserve it, while others deserve to be treated like the wantons they are.'

She turned away, feeling the terrible loss of intimacy, of the thrill of togetherness which should have characterised this moment when at last they found themselves alone . . . on their wedding night.

'Come here, Martine.' Gentle the tone but commanding. She shook her head sadly and heard him repeat the order, this time with an imperative ring which demanded obedience. She moved, graceful and lovely in her flowing white gown, orchids in her hair, a diamond necklace at her throat—Luke's wedding present given to her last evening.

'Luke . . . I . . .' She had no idea what she wanted to say, but she did know that she wanted to run from him, to seek the shelter and safety of her own little apartment.

'There's nothing to be afraid of,' he murmured, his hands capturing hers, bringing her to him, then encircling her soft young body. 'Nerves are just a product of a certain attitude of mind, which is itself born of unproductive imaginings. Fear can be very much the same.' Without giving her a chance to comment Luke bent his head and kissed her on the lips, possessively and masterfully, yet with a certain gentleness, too, as if he would reassure her that he was no ogre whose savagery she had to fear. 'Come, Martine,' he murmured, his lips moist and warm against the tender hollow of her throat. 'It's time we were in bed. You need sleep.'

'Sleep?' like a drowning man clutching at a straw. 'You mean . . . ?'

'If you prefer to be on your own tonight I'll not raise any objections.'

Relief swept over her like a deluge of warm, soothing water. She lifted her face involuntarily, offering her lips again in thanks and gratitude. 'You're kind . . . and understanding,' she breathed. 'Thank you, Luke.'

His smile was sardonic. 'It's only for tonight,' he warned. 'You know why I married you, so don't cherish any ideas that ours is to be a marriage of convenience, a marriage in name only.'

She coloured but managed to say steadily, 'I realise that this feeling I have at present is silly, and you need have no fear, Luke, that I shall expect you to—to keep away—er—all the time.'

The straight dark eyebrows lifted a fraction. 'That's as well, my dear,' he returned smoothly. 'I haven't the slightest intention of keeping away indefinitely. Haven't I just made myself clear on that score?'

She nodded. 'Yes, Luke,' and now her voice carried a meekness which came quite naturally under the present circumstances. 'You have made it clear.'

He kissed her again, gave her a little slap and told her to go to bed before he changed his mind.

She had been in her room for more than half an hour before she began to undress. What on earth was the matter with her? she wondered irritably. This was what she had wanted but had not dared to hope for—to be alone. . . .

Or was it what she had wanted? Her eyes strayed to the communicating door between her room and Luke's. Was he asleep? She had heard him moving about, had noticed the sound of water through the wall of her bathroom, which backed up to his. He had been taking a shower, she had surmised. And now there was silence. With a sigh of impatience she laid the lovely dress over the back of a chair then stood before the mirror, hands pressed to her pale cheeks. This was her wedding night and she was alone. Her thoughts went to Kelvin, and to what this night would have been but for the intrusion of Sophia into their lives. Tears gathered in Martine's eyes and she angrily brushed them away before they fell. Crying was futile. She had made a complete mess of her life with her impulsive wish for revenge. She was furious with herself, and even more furious with Luke for coming into her life at this crucial time. She hated him! She would run away first thing in the morning! Yes, she would go home to England, where she could begin to pick up the threads of her life again.

She moved nervously, knocked against a dainty Queen Anne chair and winced as it fell to the floor. But she saw with relief as she picked it up that it was not damaged. She was wide awake and, sure that sleep would elude her, she went to the window, opened it and stepped through on to the verandah. The moon was high over the sacred sanctuary, bathing the ruined temples with a soft, pearl-white glow. Gnarled olive trees took on grotesque shapes; an eagle glided and swooped and Martine closed her eyes. Some poor unsuspecting prey. . . . What had Nature been about to make it necessary for one creature to kill another in order to live? Depressed, and still unable to understand this blank despondency that had taken possession of her, this soul-searching which produced no results, she re—entered the room and crossed it. She would have a bath, she decided. A bath was always soothing, both to body and spirit. She would feel better in a few minutes.

She had come from the bathroom wrapped in a huge bath sheet and was drying herself when the communicating door opened and Luke was there, his dark blue satin dressing gown tied loosely with a matching cord. Her swift, perceptive glance assured her that he was naked beneath its covering.

'What on earth have you been doing?' he wanted to know, his black eyes stripping the towel from her still damp figure. 'You've been moving about for over an hour. What's the matter with you?'

'Nothing.' She clutched at the towel as if expecting him to drag it from her. 'I—I was just going to—to bed.'

Luke's black eyes narrowed perceptively and he came into the room, closing the door behind him. Martine's nerves tightened.

'So you've changed your mind about wanting to be alone on your wedding night,' he commented dryly. 'Haven't I always maintained that females are perverse?'

'I—please go away—'

'If you wanted your husband so much then why the devil didn't you knock on the door? I'd have come willingly.' His voice carried a ring of humour not unmingled with confidence. Martine felt her temper rise but the denial that leapt to her lips was crushed before a word was uttered. She was breathless when he released her, breathless and half-willing for him to make love to her. But she fought to retain the towel, and even when it was removed she continued to struggle until Luke threatened to put her across his knee. Only then did she desist, confident that it was no idle threat he uttered.

His dressing gown was open and their bodies, warm and supple, blended as one and almost immediately a sort of aching delight swept through her as she succumbed to the possessive exploration of his hands. Nor was his mouth idle; it pressed moistly against the hollow of her throat, sensitive to the wild pulsation of a nerve. It wandered down to press kisses on her honey-gold skin; it captured and held the dark and swollen peak of her breast.

She gave a little moan as rapture spread through her veins, digging her fingers into his back, arching her body in a wild and primitive desire for the fulfilment of a need that threatened to make her a suppliant, pleading for the ecstacy that seemed to be only a breath away. Luke was murmuring in his own language but Martine scarcely heard, affected as she was by the exquisite pain of long sinewed fingers teasing her breast while Luke's other hand pressed very different curves, compelling her to feel the virile strength and hardness of his thighs.

Every nerve-end, every cell in her body was affected, and every sense. The musky smell of his skin mingling with a severely masculine talc, the warmth of his hard frame against the softness of her own, the tactile exploration of her own eager hands. . . . All compounded to send spasms of sheer bliss spreading with explosive force through her body and with a whisper of entreaty she murmured huskily, desperate for total fulfilment, 'Love me . . . I need you. . . .'

With a throb of excitement and relief she felt herself lifted into his arms, knew the sensual rhythm of his movements as he bore her over to the big bed and laid her down.

He stood over her, sinewed and naked, shaking his head in a gesture of admonishment. 'I knew there would be a need for decisive action.'

She merely nodded, lifting her arms in a tender invitation. But for a moment he continued to look down at her, beautiful and seductive in the gentle rose-pink glow from the single lamp on the cabinet by the bed. Her long silky lashes fluttered down, casting adorable shadows on to her cheeks. His mouth curved and a glitter

entered his black eyes—the manifestation of the
power and the triumph which he knew were his.
He lay down beside her, his hands instantly
taking possession of tender places. She closed
her eyes, her breathing as ragged as his . . . and
then suddenly she belonged to him, rapture indescribable sweeping through her after the first
agonising stab of pain, rapture in all the glory of
exquisite mating, rapture that carried her to the
very heights of heaven . . . and beyond.

It was less than a fortnight later that she
realised something had gone amiss in the affair
between Kelvin and Sophia. She had been seeing them together, strolling among the temples
of the Sancturary or walking hand in hand along
the tree-lined lane which led from her father's
house to the villa where Kelvin lived and
worked. But one day Martine saw Sophia
walking in the ruins on her own, saw her sit
down and then rise again as a young Greek
approached. Sophia stretched forth her hands;
they were taken and brought to the young man's
lips. The incident had naturally set Martine
thinking but she did not mention it to her husband.

But when she happened to come across Kelvin
as she emerged from the chemist's shop in the
village she could not resist asking, 'How are
things between you and Sophia these days?'

His face was a study of dejection. 'She's rotten!' he exclaimed bitterly. 'It was just a bit of
fun for her and now she's repeating the performance with another fool!'

'Repeating the performance? Why, is he engaged?'

'There's no need for sarcasm! No, he's not, but he does have a girl friend—or he did. Sophia's one ambition seems to be the breaking up of other people's romances.'

'How is the book progressing?' inquired Martine, feeling it better to change the subject.

'It's not progressing. You know very well I can't type.'

'Anyone can type if they try.'

'My time ought to be more profitably employed than in the simple task of typing,' he returned impatiently. 'I happen to be the creative one; the typist merely puts my thoughts and findings on paper.'

'You make it sound as if my contribution had not been of much importance at all.' Martine fingered the package she was carrying, a brown paper bag containing her favourite soap which she had been pleasantly surprised to find available in the chemist's shop.

'Of course it was important,' contradicted her ex-fiancé. 'You and I worked together in a way that was unique.' He paused and all his anger seemed to melt. 'I miss you,' he said slowly. 'I miss you like the devil.'

She averted her face, unwilling to ask herself if she felt the same way, if she missed him. 'Well, there's nothing to be done about it now,' she murmured with an unconscious sigh. 'You'll find someone else—'

'Never. I know now that I made a mistake, so much so that I'm beginning to distrust all my judgements—even where they concern my work.'

A tense silence followed before Martine said, 'Are you sure that Sophia's really interested in this other man? She certainly appeared to be very attracted to you at the time—'

'She's fickle and you knew it from the first. It was I who was blind.' Martine said nothing and after a pause Kelvin went on, 'You and—and that Greek . . . you can't be in love with him. You married him for spite, didn't you?'

She could not deny that it had been something of the kind—well, partly it had been spite, as she had mentioned to Luke, spite and revenge. But there had been something more, something which was unrelated . . . desire. She had wanted Luke as a lover and she was thankful that he had offered her marriage, for she knew that she would otherwise have ended up as his mistress because the pull of his magnetism would have proved too strong for her.

Kelvin was speaking again, repeating the assertion that she was not in love with her husband, that she had married him to spite himself.

She looked up, her mouth quivering. He was still as handsome in her eyes, still someone to be admired even though she had discovered flaws in his make-up. Everyone had flaws, she thought, admitting that she had plenty herself.

'I admit I didn't love him,' she said at last.

'You couldn't very well deny it, could you?'

She shrugged. 'You said I'd been having an affair with him while I was engaged to you,' she could not help reminding him.

'I was angry. I didn't mean it; you must have known that.' He looked at her and she saw all the old familiar admiration in his eyes. Regret registered there, too, in the shadowed depths of his concentrated gaze. Martine swallowed the hard little lump that had lodged in her throat and it came as a sudden shock to her to realise she would put back the clock if she could, put it back before her wedding day. It was all so illogical, though, since she could not truthfully deny the fact that the physical pleasure she derived from her marriage was all-important to her.

'How long will it take to finish your book?' she asked, needing to cut the silence which was beginning to stretch too far.

'I can't say. Concentration's so difficult—' He stopped and there was a small hesitation before he said, 'Martine—would you do the typing for me?'

She shook her head even while her brain was considering the possibility.

'No—Luke would not allow it.'

'Allow?' he snapped. 'That is not a word I'd have expected you to use so casually!'

'Luke's—well, a little—er—bossy.'

'Domineering, you mean?' through his teeth. 'A typical Greek, is he? Lord of all he surveys, especially his womenfolk?'

'I'm not discussing my husband with you,' she said curtly. 'I had better be going anyway. It's getting towards lunch time.'

'And you dare not keep your husband waiting?' Sarcasm in the tone which would have angered Martine but that she was sorry for him.

'It isn't good manners to keep people waiting,' was all she said, but when she turned to go Kelvin fell into step beside her.

'I'm going your way,' he said, 'so we might as well walk together.'

It so happened that Luke saw them through the window of his bedroom and his face was stern and set when Martine entered the dining-room where lunch was being served.

'I saw you with Kelvin.' His voice was clipped, his mouth compressed.

'We met in the village and walked up together.'

'I'd rather you didn't walk with him. The affair's finished; you're married to me. It'll cause gossip in the village if you and he are seen together too often.'

Her eyes sparkled. Surely he did not intend to dictate to her to that extent! 'It isn't often. It was just today.'

'Then let it be the last time.' He held out a chair and she sat down, anger bringing colour to her cheeks.

'He's very upset,' she began, then stopped, reluctant to disclose that the affair with Sophia had ended so abruptly. But it transpired that Luke already knew. He, too, had seen Sophia with this other man.

'It's only what he deserves,' he declared, taking a seat opposite his wife. She looked at him, aware of his anger and guessing that he was wondering what she and Kelvin had been talking about. But, to her relief, he did not ask and so she was not forced to tell him any lies.

The following afternoon she met Kelvin again, this time on the site where he was walking about with a notebook in his hand. He saw her before she could retreat and so she strolled over and joined him by the Temple of Hera, built in the 7th century B.C. He smiled, but carried on with the taking of notes. She said, 'Hello,' feeling awkward, and it seemed years instead of a few short weeks since they had parted.

'Hello. I'm just writing a description of the scene here. You'll notice that pines and other trees have rooted among the ruins, so I suppose one could describe the area as a sort of park?'

'It certainly has a park-like appearance,' she agreed, her awkwardness dissolving as if by magic as she fell into his mood. For this was like old times and she knew a lightness of heart as she and Kelvin talked about the site and the history of one of the most famous places in Greece—in the entire world, in fact.

She glanced around her, appreciating the setting, with the Arcadian Mountains forming an impressive backdrop at one side of the valley, while to the other side was the coastal plain bordering enchanting lagoons where gaily-coloured caiques could often be seen, their owners taking full advantage of the presence of the fish that inhabited the calm, aquamarine waters. It was late summer now and the reeds were high, interspersed with castus bushes and delicate oleanders, sweet-scented, their clusters of white and cerise flowers adding magic to the scene. The sun was high but not too hot, and filmy clouds swirled about like veils of gossamer lace.

'I'm going over to the gymnasium now.' Kelvin looked at her questioningly. 'Are you coming?'

'I don't know,' hesitantly. 'I merely came out for a walk, then found myself crossing the bridge and—well, here I am.'

There were few people on the site and they had this particular area to themselves. Kelvin looked at her, noting the rare beauty of her skin, its peach-bloom transparency, smooth and glowing with health. Her hair shone in the sunlight and she looked so young, he thought, young and very lovely. She had the figure of a nymph and she was as light-footed—sometimes he used to think she walked on air. . . . Happy memories, sad thoughts. He saw her looking at him with an expression of inquiry and smiled in the old familiar way that had always brought a reponse. But today there was no response; she was serious but he felt she was not too unhappy—certainly she was not as unhappy as he.

'Are you coming?' he asked again and this time she said yes, she would come with him.

They walked slowly, passing the Prytaneum, the place where, in ancient times, exalted guests were entertained, guests who included the victors at the Games who were given a glorious banquet in their honour. Reaching the Gymnasium they stopped and Martine found herself looking up, towards the Villa Cladeos, and her heart gave an involuntary jerk at the possibility of her husband being able to see her. But she felt that, even were he on the terrace, he would not be able to see her so far away, here among the bushes and trees.

'Would you like me to take some notes for you, Kelvin? I might as well, seeing that I'm here.'

'I'd be grateful for any help you'd care to give.' He handed her the book in which he had been writing and pulled another from his pocket.

She took the pencil and began to make notes. 'You merely want descriptions?'

'Yes—the atmosphere as you feel it, standing here, with the warm sun on your face and the river flowing and glistening in its rays.'

She began to write, forgetful of all but the

work in hand. And although she wrote only descriptions and impressions her mind was partly in the far distant past when the full glory of Greece was at its zenith, when the Olympic Games were a sacred truce which brought all wars to an end, when the aggressive, brawling tribes gathered together to engage in athletics and to worship the sacred Olympian deities. The competitors came from near and far—from Italy and Asia Minor, from Egypt, and in fact from every part of the known world. To the Greeks a virile, healthy body was of paramount importance because they believed it made for an equally healthy mind. It was here at Olympia, before man competed against man, that the gods fought one another—Zeus wrestling with Kronos, his father, to gain the kingdom of the world, and the son of Zeus, Apollo, competing with the god Hermes in a very special race which the Sun god eventually won.

'How are you getting on?' Kelvin's voice was close; she felt his breath on her cheek.

'I'm doing fine, I think.' She moved away, remembering that in days not too far gone she would have turned to Kelvin, offering her lips for his kiss.

'You seemed to be a long way off.'

'As a matter of fact, I was. Somewhere around seven hundred years before Christ.'

He managed a laugh then and said, 'The Olympiads.'

'I have just remembered that women were totally barred from the Games. It earned them the death penalty if they even entered the site.'

'But one managed to take on the disguise of a trainer and was for a long time undiscovered.'

'Yes, I remember! But she wept when one of her sons won a race.'

'Her tears gave her away.'

'But she was pardoned because she had so many victors in her family.'

'That's right. Though after that the judges decreed that all trainers and athletes had to be naked.' He grinned at her. 'That effectively put a stop to any intrusions by women.'

She laughed but reminded him that women were, later, allowed to compete. Ten minutes later she looked at her watch and gave a little gasp. 'We've been here for more than an hour and a half! It seems more like twenty minutes!'

'Time flies when you're content.' He had moved close again and he took her hand in his. 'Martine, what are we to do?'

'There isn't anything—'

'You don't love Luke and he doesn't love you.' He paused, as if undecided, but then added resolutely, 'I know why he married you, and I suppose you do too?'

She nodded after a small pause and said yes, she knew why Luke had married her. 'We were two people drawn together by a grudge,' she admitted. 'He had a grudge against Sophia's sister and I had one against you.'

'What a basis for marriage! I said you were mad.'

'Who told you about Luke's reason for marrying me?' she asked, ignoring the outburst. 'Was it Sophia?'

'Sophia did mention it first, but—I've seen Odette. Sophia introduced me to her.'

'Odette?' Martine felt her merves tense. 'Is she here in Olympia?'

'She's on a prolonged visit to her father. She normally lives in Athens, in a luxury apartment just outside the city.'

Odette here. . . . 'Odette told you she'd once been engaged to Luke?'

'Yes, and she admitted she'd made the mistake of her life when she threw him over. This other man she married seems to have been a near brute.'

'I've met Odette, too,' Martine informed him. 'She was in the hotel where we were dining.'

'She did mention it,' he said.

Martine shot him a glance, her eyes intent. There was something strange about him all at once; it was if he were affected in some way by the turn the conversation had taken. Something made her say, 'Have you seen Odette just the once?'

He hesitated and then, 'I've spoken with her several times.'

'You—you aren't attracted to her, are you?'

'I'm attracted to you and always will be.'

'But I'm married!'

'Marriages can be terminated. Odette says it's simple.'

'What makes you suppose I should want my marriage terminated?'

'I believe you still care for me,' he returned seriously.

'It's too late,' she quivered, torn suddenly by the bleakness of his expression. 'Oh, Kelvin, what made you do it?' She felt almost distraught and wished she had not come here. The atmosphere, the knowledge of being in the abode of ancient gods and heroes, the setting and the sanctity . . . She turned to him and placed her hand upon his arm. 'It really is too late, Kelvin, ' she whispered brokenly. 'I'm married and that's the end of it.'

'We'll see,' was his grim rejoinder. 'You love me and I love you and so we ought to do something about getting together again—and this time,' he said, bending and kissing her quivering lips, 'it'll be for keeps. I've learned the lesson of my life, Martine, and from now on you can put your full trust in my integrity.'

Chapter Five

Martine stood on the terrace looking down at the couple standing on the bank of the river and her eyes narrowed. It was Kelvin and Odette, standing close as if in intimate conversation.

She turned as her husband joined her; she saw his glance dart to the Sanctuary, knew he, too, had seen the couple by the river—the River Cladeos after which the villa was named.

He began to frown and his mouth went tight. 'It would seem that your ex-fiancé is consoling himself already,' he remarked, nothing in his tone to reveal what was in his mind. 'Did you know he was acquainted with Odette?'

Was Luke jealous? wondered Martine with a tinge of dejection.

'He mentioned it yesterday—'

'You were with him yesterday!' sharply and with a swift gleam of anger in his eyes.

'We came across one another on the site,' she answered, keeping her voice steady even while her heart was beginning to beat a little faster than normal. 'Odette told him why you married me.'

A sneer molded Luke's underlip, but he made no reference to what Martine had said. 'I told you not to see Kelvin again.' He regarded his wife sternly. 'My wishes are not to be ignored, Martine. You must learn that when I say a thing I mean it.'

Her chin lifted. 'I won't be dictated to, Luke! There is no harm in my talking to Kelvin.'

'Perhaps not,' tersely but still with that authoritative inflection. 'I was not speaking about harm but about my wishes. You will keep away from this man; do you understand?'

'No, I do not understand!'

'You're defying me?'

She swallowed, angry that her heart was now almost racing. He could scare her, this dark Greek whom she had married with such impulsive haste. Nevertheless, she adopted a brave mien as she said, looking directly at him, 'I did not take on a master when I married you—'

'But you did,' was the smoothly-spoken interruption. 'In Greece, the husband *is* the master. The sooner you accept this the better it will be for you.'

She paled with anger. To be spoken to like this! She wanted to hit him, wanted to convince him in some way that he could not domineer over her because she was English, not one of his meek and docile countrywomen whose lot it was to be servile all their lives. But she did and said nothing, because Luke was occupied all at once by the couple below, his whole attention caught, and as she followed the direction of his gaze she saw that the couple were shaking hands, as if sealing a bargain. . . .

Luke startled her by saying, suspicion and curiosity affecting the depth and tone of his voice, 'I wonder what those two are up to? It savours of a conspiracy.'

'That's exactly the impression I had—' Martine pulled herself up abruptly, not having meant to voice her opinion like that.

Luke turned to stare down into her face. 'Have you any ideas, then?' he wanted to know.

She shook her head. 'None. I think perhaps we are imagining things.'

'Perhaps,' he agreed but there was that in his tone which convinced Martine that his suspicions were still there.

'I think I'll go in,' she murmured.

'This matter of your seeing Kelvin,' he said, before she could move. 'I meant what I said, Martine.'

'He'll be gone soon.' She recalled her feelings of yesterday and wondered if she would miss Kelvin when he left. She was very conscious of the fact that there was a spiritual aspect to her love for Kelvin, and already she was beginning to realise that marriage without it lacked something so vital that doubts were slowly creeping into her mind. She threw them off, hoping they would not recur. But they did, faintly at present but she suspected those doubts would increase in strength until they had an adverse affect on her relationship with her husband.

'Meanwhile,' said Luke firmly, 'you will obey my orders and not see him again.'

'Orders!' she blazed.

'It would seem that an order is necessary.'

'It will be disobeyed!'

'At your peril.' There was a merciless quality

about him which impelled Martine to raise a
barrier of caution, much to her chagrin.

'Shall we let the matter drop, Luke? It's un-
likely that Kelvin and I shall run across one
another very often. He works in his room most of
the time.'

'He works on the site almost every day.'

Had Luke been watching for him? Martine
dismissed the idea, feeling it was more likely
that Luke had merely noticed Kelvin wandering
in the Sanctuary, for he went early, before the
tourists invaded with their multi-lingual guides,
their cameras and their orange peel.

'I don't feel like keeping off the site,' she said.
'It draws me with its atmosphere of bygone
splendour, its setting and the perfect peace I feel
when I wander about among the ruins. The
ancient Greeks certainly knew how to choose
their locations.'

He nodded, catching her mood as his eyes
roamed to the site again. The couple had disappeared and there was no one on the river's edge.
Martine could almost smell the perfume of the
oleanders flourishing on the banks, hear the
drone of the cicadas, the sweet tinkling of sheep
and goat bells from the lush green foothills of
the mountains.

'You like it here?' Luke barred her way when
she would have moved.

'The place? I adore it.'

'You've no regrets?' His black eyes wandered
to the place where the couple had stood and she
knew instinctively that his mind was on Kelvin,
not Odette.

'Not . . . really.'

'Why the hesitation?' His voice was suddenly
harsh.

'I feel that I might have regrets later—' She stopped. 'I don't want to talk about it,' she added and, brushing past him, she ran into the house and up to her room.

Kelvin and Odette. . . . Martine bit her lip. A conspiracy. . . . No, there could not be anything like that between them. It was something else, perhaps more intimate. But only yesterday Kelvin had denied feeling anything for Odette. . . . Nevertheless Martine knew a stab of jealousy, and felt she must see Kelvin as soon as possible.

She stiffened as the door between her room and Luke's swung inwards. 'I promised to take you to Mykonos,' he said without preamble. 'We'll go tomorrow.'

'This is sudden.'

'We haven't had a honeymoon.'

She looked at him suspiciously. 'You want to get me away from Kelvin, don't you?'

His mouth compressed; he came towards her. 'I have no need to "get you away" as you term it. My word is law and you'll regard it!'

'And if I don't?' The colour had drained from her cheeks and her nerves tensed as she waited for him to speak.

'You might or might not know that in Greece a man is allowed to beat his wife.'

'You'd not beat me,' she returned but her confidence was feigned, the result of assumed bravado rather than defiance.

'Don't try me too hard,' he advised. 'I'm not over-endowed with patience.' He was close; she felt instinctively that he was inhaling the heady yet delicate aroma of the perfume she wore. A sense of expectancy invaded her as she lifted her face to scrutinise his expression. 'No, don't try me too hard,' he said again. 'I wouldn't want to do anything to mar the very satisfactory relationship we have.'

His hands caught hers and she was brought close, her breath coming swiftly as the blood surged to her heart. How easily his magnetism could affect her! He had said she was putty in his hands and she had to agree that he was right. His mouth come down, possessing hers in a long and ardent kiss that left her gasping for breath. His hands moved slowly from her waist down her spine and her senses quickened with the warmth of perception. He was going to make love to her.

She made no attempt to fight him; on the contrary, every erotic nerve in her body became affected by the exquisite prompting of his hands. They created a delicious invigoration within her; she was invaded by his ardour as he possessed her curves, curling his fingers in sensual readiness to take the weight of her body. When he lifted her she let her head fall on to his shoulder, taking a passive delight in what he was doing to her. He stood her by the bed and unbuttoned her blouse, pausing then to caress her breasts through the fine lace of their scanty covering.

His face was close, his breath cool and clean on her cheek. 'Just you remember, always, that you are mine,' he said almost harshly and lifted her on to the bed.

It was evening when they arrived on Mykonos. They came by ferry from Piraeus, having spent the previous night in Athens. A small caique had landed them not far from their hotel, the Leto, where their room had a wonderful view of the harbour and the dark waters of the Aegean

Sea. Martine's first impression was of gleaming white cubic houses and equally immaculate churches, of windmills which used to turn in the breeze—the *meltimi*—'wind of the islands'. Only one mill was in use now, Luke had told her.

After dinner they strolled on the waterfront and Martine listened with rapt attention as her husband explained the mythology of the island.

'It's supposed to be the rock tomb of one of the victims of Herakles, and the body of Ajax the smaller was also buried here.'

'It all sounds so true,' she said with a wry smile. 'I can't always take it in that it is pure fiction.'

'To the ancient Greeks it wasn't fiction.'

'Their lives were ruled by the gods, weren't they?'

He nodded. 'Just as, today, the lives of the Balinese peoples—and lots of others—are ruled by the gods.'

'Man seems always to have had something to believe in, to cling to.'

Luke nodded his agreement but said nothing. The stroll was slow and companionable, with Martine's hand in his and her slender body close. After awhile they came to a *taverna* where several men were dancing to the strains of a *bouzouki* band and Luke stopped.

'Would you like a drink?' he asked and Martine instantly agreed. They went in and were shown to a table where they could enjoy the spectacle of the dancing. Luke had Turkish coffee in a minute cup, along with the inevitable glass of iced water, while Martine drank lemonade. Others around them were drinking *ouzo*, along with plates of *mezédes*—bits of smoked octopus and olives and diced cucumber. The atmosphere was light and casual, the Mykoniats smiling periodically at the tourists who came in, smiling encouragement, Luke remarked, amused.

'The people of this island especially like the tourists. They'll do anything for them.'

'They bring money to the island.'

'It was not so long ago that this place was the most notorious of the Cyclades. It was the favoured haunt of the jet set and bathing in the nude was common. Also, there was much indecent dress, but things have improved and the nudists keep to the official naturalist beaches.'

Martine coloured as he spoke, feeling she would rather die than bathe in the nude. Watching her in some amusement Luke said with a laugh, 'We are living in modern times, my dear.'

'All the same . . .' Her eyes glittered with a challenge. 'All the same, you'd not like me to—to swim with nothing on.'

'Not like it?' with a swift lift of his brows. 'I'd never allow it.' He looked at her, his chiselled mouth taut and hard.

She would like to have found some fitting retort but as none came she changed the subject, asking him about the tiny island of Delos which they were to visit on the morrow, leaving the pier in a *caique* at nine o'clock.

'Tell me about the mythology,' she urged.

He smiled then and the grim inflexibility of his mouth relaxed. 'It began, as so many of the Greek legends began, with the amorous exploits of that most lusty of all gods, Zeus—'

'Of course,' she broke in, laughing. 'He had been chasing some reluctant maiden—as usual?'

'Asteria, who ran from him, adopting the form of a quail. So Zeus became an eagle. But Asteria turned into a rock and fell into the sea. This rock was called Adelos, which means the Invisible One, and it moved about just beneath the surface for a long time. Meanwhile Zeus pursued her sister, Leto, taking on the form of a swan— What are you laughing at?'

'Nothing! I love it! Carry on!'

'Up loomed the inevitable Hera, Zeus's wife— who always did loom up, to spoil things.' It was Luke who was laughing now while Martine frowned her impatience as she waited for him to continue. 'Hera told Mother Earth to prevent the tragic Leto from having her offspring anywhere on earth, and so Leto became a wanderer, unable to give birth because all places feared the wrath of Hera.'

He paused a moment, as if in thought, and Martine said, 'What about Zeus? He was allpowerful, so why didn't he help her?'

'Ah, yes! As a matter of fact, he did, by asking his brother to do something, which Poseidon did, anchoring the isle of Adelos with four diamond columns. So Adelos the Invisible became Delos the Visible.

'An enchanting story,' sighed Martine. 'Oh, but I adore these tales of ancient Greece. Leto had her child on the island of Delos, then?'

'Twins,' corrected Luke with a smile. 'First came the female, the goddess Artemis, patron of the hunt and goddess of virginity. Nine days later Apollo the Sun god was born and a great light shone over the isle of Delos.'

'So Delos, like Delphi, became involved with the cult of Apollo?'

'That's right.'

'I'm going to enjoy our trip tomorrow!' Martine's thought went to Kelvin, whom she knew

would love to include Delos in his book. She
must mention it to him when next she saw him.
She had been pondering the possibility of doing
his typing for him and when, later, Luke said he
would be away in Athens for a couple of days the
following week she decided this would give her
the opportunity she wanted.

Delos proved to be all she had imagined, and
much more. Once the rather rough two-mile
journey by caique had been made, the harbour
was calm, the island opening out like a fan
rising to a rocky peak which gleamed bright in
the sun. The ghost of a Roman city was evident
in the rows of broken columns near the harbour.
Freed Roman slaves once lived here, Luke told
her. The road to the Sanctuary of Apollo—the
Sacred Way—had in ancient times been lined
with glorious statues but, sadly, there was only
scant evidence left—fragments of the lovely columns where dozens of giant lizards basked in
the warm sun, their bodies stock still, their
senses alert to danger so that when anyone came
too close they were off like a shot.

'The gateway to this Sanctuary was built of
white marble,' a guide was saying quietly. 'It
dates from two centuries before Christ.'

There were three Temples to Apollo, built at
different times. There was the Tomb of the
Virgins—maidens who assisted Leto in the birth
of her twins; there was the Temple of Leto
herself, and numerous other intriguing temples
and of course the Stadium and Gymnasium
found on most ancient sites of this kind. All were
in ruins, with poppies galore spreading vivid
colour among the crevices and between the
fallen and broken columns.

In the one-time residential quarters the impressive House of the Dolphins and the House of the Masks were to be seen, with wells or cisterns beneath the floor, and often sewage systems.

'They were so artistic, weren't they?' Martine was staring down at the lovely mosaics covering one floor in the House of the Dolphins where cupids rode on the dolphins' backs, holding symbols alluding to various gods—the trident for Poseidon, god of the sea, the thyrsus for Dionysos, and another which had been destroyed and so was not identifiable.

'The Greeks are still artistic.'

'Not as much as they were in ancient times.'

'The craftsmen then had more time at their disposal, I expect.'

The House of the Masks was especially rich in mosaics and Martine and Luke stayed a long while enjoying the rich representations of amphorae, palm trees, birds and rosettes, a dancer and a flute player, the god Dionysos riding on a panther and, of course, the grandeur of the Masks after which the house was named. Moving on, they came to the Theatre, where over five thousand spectators could be accommodated, giving some idea of the tiny island's population in those far-off days.

The House of the Trident was another beautiful attraction for the tourists who had come, along with Martine and Luke, in the caique.

'It obviously had a rich owner,' Martine observed, her rapt attention on the wondrous mosaic where a Panathenaic Amphora was depicted. Painted upon it was the figure of a chariot, while adorning it were a palm tree and a wreath of olive leaves.

'These mean that the owner's family had won

a victory, or victories in the Panathanaic Games.' Luke pointed to the wreath especially. 'Often the wreath was of laurel leaves.'

'And that was the only prize?'

He nodded. 'The glory of winning was considered sufficient without any valuable reward.'

'They had high ideals.'

He shrugged his shoulders, smiling faintly. 'They had no compunction about killing one another once the Games were over. Don't forget, the tribes of ancient Greece were no different from the nations of the world today. They had a thirst for war.'

'It's hard to understand. I mean, they were so devout.'

'In their pagan way, yes, they were,' he agreed, taking her arm and moving away towards the House of Dionysos, where lovely wall carvings had been preserved for many centuries. They depicted mainly triremes. The mosaic showing the winged Dionysos riding a tiger was so lovely that Martine, used though she now was to the beauty, gave a little gasp of admiration. 'What a lovely variety of stones they used! Just look at the different colours!'

But it was the sacred lions, silhouetted against the azure Grecian sky, that Martine remembered most vividly. Sixteen of these Naxian marble monuments had once existed, flanking a terrace and guarding the sacred lake where the ancients obtained their water. Sadly, only five lions now remained.

'It was wonderful,' sighed Martine, when at last they were on their way back to the boat. They had climbed Mt. Cynthus, had wandered among countless fragments of temples and houses, while from the bushes birds sang and from among the grasses came the soft, sweet tinkle of sheep bells, for the farmers of Mykonos sometimes brought their sheep here to graze. 'Thank you, Luke, for bringing me.' She smiled up at him, yet there came the unbidden image of Kelvin, who would love this place, because, like her, he had let himself become steeped in the history of ancient Greece.

'It's been a pleasure.' Luke took her hand; she felt his thumb caressing her smooth, honey-gold skin and a quiver shot through her at his action. Undoubtedly the physical aspect of their relationship was as vital to her as it was to him. Yet what must be the end of it? she wondered, feeling there could not possibly be any permanency in the marriage. One or the other of them would decide there was too much lacking once the newness of the physical attraction had worn off, which it must, she thought, without anything to support it.

They were back on Mykonos for lunch, which they took in one of the *tavernas* along the sea road in downtown Mykonos and afterwards they spent a few enjoyable hours on the beach at Aghios Stephanos, where they alternately swam and sunned themselves and talked of the trip they had made to Delos.

The following day they took a trip to Ano Mera where the famous Tourliani Monastery was situated. Its steeple was of sculptured marble, gleaming in the sun. A monk came to them as they entered the monastery and insisted on showing them an icon supposedly painted by St Luke.

'It ees of the miraculous,' he asserted from behind his long flowing beard. 'It cures many kind of illness—no?'

Luke put some money in the box and they left, much to the disgust of the monk, who had been exceedingly interested in Martine's figure, appearing to be quite unable to take his eyes off her curves, especially her breasts. His eyes seemed to be glued to them and she found herself blushing, while her husband's eyes glinted and his mouth went tight.

'Greek monks are all the same,' he snapped as they left. 'Why the devil they even become monks in the first place has always been a mystery to me!'

Martine had to laugh, but when this produced an even broader scowl on Luke's face she instantly became serious again.

Woe betide her, she mused with an involuntary shiver, if she should ever give this Greek husband of hers cause for jealousy.

Chapter Six

Martine stood on the terrace watching Luke's Mercedes as it travelled smoothly along the road. It was soon out of sight and she turned, half wishing he had asked her to accompany him to Athens. Yet on the other hand she was experiencing a strange excitement at her freedom for a few days . . . freedom to go back to her apartment, and to see Kelvin and perhaps clear up the neglected typing he had mentioned. Luke had said he would be away for about three days but he would phone her anyway, to let her know when he was hoping to be back. From what little he had mentioned he had several meetings to attend and various other business to see to, so Martine estimated he would be away for the better part of the week.

She went immediately to the villa where Kelvin lived and found him in, sitting in a rather forlorn pose on the verandah, a notebook and pencil in his hands. His eyes lit up when he saw her and he rose instantly, dropped pencil and book on the table and held out both his hands.

Slowly she put hers into them, feeling uneasy and yet at the same time glad she was here. It was all so illogical; she could not understand herself. It seemed that she desired the spiritual love she had shared with Kelvin *and* the physical pleasure provided by her husband. She felt almost immoral!

'You look lovely, my dear.' Kelvin's voice held all the old familiar admiration, but it was tinged with regret, too, and his mouth quivered slightly.

'Thank you.' As on the other occasion, she felt awkward and spoke swiftly in an effort to ease. the situation. 'I thought, that as Luke's away for a few days, I'd come down and see what I could do to help you.'

'He's away—for a few days?'

'That's right.'

'I'm glad you've come. I tried to phone you but was told you were away from home.'

'We went to Mykonos—oh, Kelvin, you'd be in your element in Delos! It's one incredible archaeological site—the whole island, I mean! No one lives there except the people who care for it. You'd be in your element,' she said again, eyes bright with the memories of all she had seen.

'I've already decided to include it in my book.' He paused and Martine asked him what he had wanted to see her about. He hesitated, and somehow she felt it was for effect rather than what it was purported to be—uncertainty as to how to begin. 'Well, it—it was about something Odette told me a few days ago—'

'Odette? You've seen her again?' Naturally her mind flew to the scene which both she and Luke had witnessed, when Kelvin and Odette had been talking on the site, and both Martine

and her husband had had the same impression
—that there seemed to be a conspiracy afoot.

'I've seen her once or twice recently,' he admitted. Another pause and then he added, looking away, towards Mt. Kronian, the wooded hill
rising above the site, 'She told me how your—
husband got that scar.'

'Yes?' Martine felt her nerves tighten as she
waited for him to continue.

'You'll not like what you're going to hear,' he
prepared her and she felt her skin prickle along
her spine.

'But you want me to hear it all the same?'

'I feel you should.'

'Then why the delay?'

'It's not as though you love your husband. . . .'
Kelvin was muttering to himself, his eyes still
avoiding hers. 'So it'll not hurt you in any way.'

'Shall we get it over and done with?' Her voice
was calm, but her nerves were tensed within
her, creating an uncomfortable tightness around
her heart.

'He got the scar in a brawl, a brawl with two
men who attacked him—' Kelvin broke off and
paused; again Martine had the impression that
it was all for effect. 'The men were brothers of a
girl he'd seduced—a peasant girl living here, in
Olympia—'

'A girl Luke had seduced?' broke in Martine
swiftly, quite unable to imagine her husband
conducting his amorous affairs so near home.

'Yes. Her name's Litsa Katsellis. Her son is
eight years old.'

'Her . . . son?' Martine's voice was hollow, her
eyes disbelieving. 'You mean—Luke's son?'

Kelvin nodded. 'It was after hearing about
that that Odette threw him over—although she

now wishes she hadn't. She admits it was a mistake.' Kelvin met her eyes at last. 'I feel she was right, though. It's disgraceful—and terribly embarrassing for a wife to know that one of her husband's children—illegitimate children, mind —lives so close. Perhaps you've even seen the child, many times and not known who he is. Odette was in ignorance at first, until someone told her the story. Did you never ask how he got the scar?'

'No—it didn't seem the thing to talk about.' Luke's son, living in the village . . . Martine frowned and shook her head. 'I don't believe this story,' she decided, looking straight at him. 'It can't possibly be true!'

'Are you suggesting your husband was a celibate until he married you?'

She blushed and her frown deepened. 'No Greek could be. I know he has had women, but it isn't feasible that he'd bring a village girl into disgrace. Why, every man knows what that poor girl would suffer. If she has a child then it must be someone else's!'

'What about the scar?'

'There could be a dozen ways in which he got it!'

'He got it, Martine, in the way I described. Odette wouldn't lie—I'm sure of it.' Again he looked away, to the lizards sunning themselves on the hot concrete floor of the verandah.

'I still don't believe it. You say Odette wouldn't lie? Well, I can't agree with you there, Kelvin. I disliked her the moment I met her and I believe she *would* lie, though for what reason I cannot possibly imagine, unless it is spite against Luke for marrying me. She had asked him if he would have her back—'

'And so he married you. He had to safeguard himself against falling for her again.' A twisted, humourless smile hovered on his lips. 'As for your not being able to find a reason why Odette should lie—well, there just isn't one, is there?'

'I mentioned spite,' she reminded him.

'Odette isn't like that, Martine, no matter what your first impression of her was. She's a charming girl and I can very well understand Luke falling madly in love with her. I guess it wouldn't take much to make him fall in love with her again.'

Martine was silent. She felt a deep dejection of spirits at what Kelvin had said. 'I guess you're right; it wouldn't take much to make him fall in love with her again.'

Odette certainly was beautiful; this Martine could never deny. But surely Luke could see that the beauty was no more than a thin veneer? Luke. . . . Was it possible that he had seduced that village girl? Martine could not ask him, but she could ask the girl herself.

Kelvin was speaking, saying he hoped she was not too upset by the story. 'It can't hurt, seeing that you don't love Luke, but it's embarrassing—'

'You had no need to tell me,' she cut in almost angrily.

'You'd have heard it in the village sometime,' he stated. 'And I felt it would be better coming from me. What are you going to do about it?' he queried after a pause.

'Do?' She intended to seek out this girl and by some subtle means ask the question which just had to be asked. But Martine had no intention of letting Kelvin know what was in her mind. 'What would you expect me to do?'

'Martine. . . .' He took her hands again. 'You and I—we love each other, need each other. Come back to me, darling, and stay forever.'

Bitterness curved her lips. 'I've already said it's too late.'

'But you don't want to remain with Luke now that you know what a rotter he is. That scar's going to be a constant reminder of his wickedness. I know and understand you, Martine, and so I know that what I say is true: that scar won't let you forget even if you wanted to, which probably you don't, seeing that you have no love for the man.'

She looked at him and for an unguarded moment fell in with his mood, comparing a future with Luke and one with Kelvin. She and he had been so happy, loving deeply no matter what Luke said to the contrary. Yes, they had really loved, had planned a wonderful future. Then Kelvin had had one small lapse. . . . She sighed, wondering why she was willing to call it a small lapse when it had caused such heartache and had been the cause of her marrying without love on either side. Love. . . . She saw that it was very possible that Luke would fall for Odette again, just as Kelvin had suggested he might.

'Darling,' he said softly, drawing her to him and enfolding her in his arms, 'come to me. Ask your husband for a divorce—'

'Kelvin, I can't! We're only just married—'

'So much the better. End it before a child comes. It would be much more difficult then.'

She shook her head, wishing she could think more clearly. But being close like this, knowing the familiar warmth and comfort of his body, the gentleness of his arms . . . she found she did not want to think about anything but the love she had for him, and the love he had for her. What was one small slip? Sophia was so lovely and appealing that she would turn the head of any man, just as her elder sister would.

Kelvin bent his head and kissed her on the lips, murmuring as he drew away at last, 'Dearest Martine, let me love you. . . .' His voice trailed off strangely and the next moment he had thrust her away, his eyes dark with anger. Swiftly Martine shot about—and stood facing the nymph-like figure of the girl who had been in her thoughts.

'Sophia!' she gasped, hot colour rising in her cheeks. 'How long have you been there?'

'Long enough,' with what could only be described as a quirk of triumph. 'So you two are back to square one—but now you have a husband, Martine. What are you going to do about that?'

'Get out!' ordered Kelvin, white fury in his face. 'What the devil are you doing here anyway?'

'I came to see you,' she answered with a pert smile. 'I never expected to break in on a little love scene like this. I—er—wonder what Luke is going to say—'

'You wouldn't tell him!'

'I might.' She threw him a challenging look. 'Why shouldn't I tell him of his wife's amorous exploits when he's away?'

Martine could only stare in contempt, remembering what Kelvin had said about Sophia's desire to ruin other people's lives. But fear was present, too, causing Martine's heart to throb wildly against her ribs and moisture to ooze from her forehead and the palms of her hands.

Yes, she was agonisingly afraid of what her husband would do if Sophia should decide to tell him of this little scene.

And Martine felt almost sure that she would tell him. . . .

Better to go away with Kelvin, if he was willing to take her away, which she felt he would be, under these present circumstances.

'You'd not be so rotten, Sophia!'

'Kelvin, darling, of course I'd be so "rotten" as you call it. I don't think it rottenness, though; I believe I would be doing Luke a good turn for, after all, why should he remain in ignorance of his wife's infidelity?'

Kelvin took a step towards her, wild fury in his gaze. 'Don't you dare use that word! There was no question of infidelity—'

'You were asking Martine to let you make love to her, and from what I could see she'd not have needed much persuasion.'

Martine's colour increased but she did not intend to enter into a slanging match with this girl who, not being satisfied with breaking up her engagement, was now contemplating breaking up her marriage.

Well, let her. Martine was suddenly aware of a draining within her, a deflation of spirit. Fate would decide what was to be the outcome of all this, and nothing could combat Fate.

Martine went down to the village after walking from the verandah, leaving the other two to talk it out if they wished. Kelvin had called after her, then followed for a few yards. She had begged him to leave her; she wanted to be alone to think. He had obeyed her wish but said he would phone her later.

The *cafeneion* was busy with tourists and locals but Martine managed a word with Marco, the proprietor. He looked at her strangely when she asked him where Litsa Kastellis lived.

'You want to talk with Litsa, no?'

'I do, yes, Marco.'

Marco gave that elaborate shrug of the shoulders which was now so familiar to Martine. It seemed to speak volumes and yet she often wondered if it meant anything at all or was merely a habit, like the twirling and clicking of the worry beads.

He gave her Litsa's address and she left the cafe. She knew the lane and he had said it was the third house on the left, the one with the bougainvillaea round the door.

The house seemed lost, unoccupied, except that there were the usual conglomeration of tins and other containers with flowers spilling out of them. Martine knocked and when she received no answer she went round to the back. Lemons shone green and bright among the darker green of the leaves; a goat was tethered to a post, the ground all around it bare and sandy. In a small clearing among the lemon trees a tired-looking donkey brayed and pawed the bare ground. Poverty seemed to characterise the whole sad place, and yet when the girl, Litsa, arrived from somewhere in the *perivoli* she was smartly clad in a printed cotton dress with a blue sash to match the cornflowers on her dress. Very dark, with expressive brown eyes and gleaming black hair, she possessed an appeal which, though very different from that of Sophia or of Odette, would certainly catch a man's attention.

'Do you know who I am?' questioned Martine

when the girl, having reached her, put down the pail she had been carrying and which Martine saw was half filled with lemons—green lemons because in Greece a yellow lemon is a 'sick lemon' according to the people who grow them.

'You are the wife of Mr. Leoros.' The girl lowered her long lashes as she spoke and Martine was reminded somehow, and for no reason she could have explained, of the way in which Kelvin had avoided her eyes earlier when he was telling her about the girl and her child.

'That's right.' Martine glanced around. 'Are you alone?'

'My mother is resting and Grandmother also.' The accent was pronounced but not as strong as Martine would have expected.

'And your little boy?'

Faintly, the girl coloured. 'He is at school.'

'His—his—father. . . .' Martine trailed off to silence and frowned. Why hadn't she rehearsed something? It wasn't as if she had not been aware that the question she wanted to ask would cause her some trouble.

However, Litsa seemed more than ready to help her out. It was almost as if she had expected a visit from Luke's wife! The idea staggered Martine, who shook off the impression, telling herself she was being fanciful.

'Mr. Leoros—the papa of my little Ulysses. I think this is what you have come to find out?'

Martine coloured up; never in her life had she felt so embarrassed, so lost for something to say. At last she managed to speak, to say in a voice little above a whisper, 'My—my husband is—is the father of Ulysses?' How she got the words out she would never know, but once having voiced them she was able to look the Greek girl in the eye, and wait for her answer with a calm she would never have believed possible.

'I have said so, Madam Leoros.'

Martine was silent, biting her lip. Suddenly she seemed to be floating on wings of unreality, telling herself that this was not happening to her, that her husband was far too honourable to besmirch the character of a village girl, a lovely girl like Litsa. For he would have been well aware that no one in the village would marry her, even had the child not come along. In fact, Martine had heard that a girl would be whipped by her father and brothers if she so much as walked with a boy before marriage.

Yet Luke had seduced the girl. . . . By her own admission he was the father of her child. Again Martine had the sensation of unreality; her thoughts were chaotic, for she did not know what to think. Yet the truth was there, stark and admitted by the girl concerned. At last Martine was able to ask, 'Does Mr. Leoros give you money?'

'He does, for me and my child. He is generous. He buy this land so we can grow many lemons and tomatoes.'

Again Martine glanced around, diverted for the moment as she said with a frown, 'You seem to be short of water, though.'

'We are not short, but we are very careful with it. You have to have much water for the lemons.'

Martine brought her attention back to the girl. She noticed now that Litsa seemed faintly ill-at-ease and this impression was strengthened when the girl said, in a voice edged with urgency and apology, 'I must go now, if you please. I have work to do in the house.'

Martine merely nodded and, turning slowly, walked away, skirting the orchard to take the narrow path along which she had approached the back of the house.

As promised Kelvin phoned her. He asked if she still wanted to help him.

'Yes, I'll do your typing for you.'

'Thanks a lot. Are you coming down now?'

'In a few minutes.' She did not know why she wanted another few minutes alone; she had been sitting on the balcony of her room, thinking as she stared unseeingly down to the Sanctuary, thinking and planning, changing her mind a dozen times, often asking herself why she should mind so much that her husband had done this vile thing to Litsa. She did not love him so she ought not to be brooding like this, wondering how she was to tell him that their marriage was finished. The next moment she was denying it was finished, then the next again she was seeing life with Kelvin, a happy life based on far more than sexual attraction.

A deep and shuddering sigh escaped her; she wished her thoughts would become clear, so that she could make a decision which she could keep to.

At length she went down to see Kelvin. He was waiting and she asked how long Sophia had stayed.

'She left about five minutes after you did,' he answered, an anxious look on his face. 'You were so upset, dear, and I didn't like letting you go.'

'I went to the village to see Litsa.' Her face was pale, her nerves taut, but her voice was calm and steady as she continued, 'It's true. Luke is the father of her child.'

They were in the sunlit living-room and Kelvin turned away abruptly, saying he would make a cup of tea. It seemed a strange thing to do—to turn so swiftly, without commenting on what she had said. 'I shan't be long,' he called from the kitchen. 'You can read through what I've written and ask any questions you consider necessary before you start to type.'

Walking over to the desk she took up a pile of papers, but her perusal was not concentrated and after a few minutes she realized she had not read a word.

'Did Sophia still persist in her intention of telling Luke?'

'I think I persuaded her to keep silent, at least for the present. I was going to tell you all about it, later.'

'You managed. . . .' Why hadn't Kelvin spoken of this at once, to put her mind at rest? Was it because her own information had erased it from his mind temporarily? 'How did you manage it?' she wanted to know, impatiently dropping the sheets of paper back on to the desk. She did not feel like doing his typing after all.

'I appealed to her better nature.'

'So she has a better nature? You surprise me.' Martine walked to the kitchen door and stood there, watching him prepare a tray with crockery and milk and sugar. 'Kelvin, I could be imagining it but—there seems some mystery to me—'

'Mystery?' in a swift interruption. 'What do you mean?'

'I can't put my finger on anything. This business of Sophia—she was so determined to talk to Luke.'

'Well, so I thought, too, but I talked to her and after a moment or two she agreed to leave it for awhile.'

'Why "for awhile"?'

'I don't know,' he replied in an expressionless voice. 'She just said that and I had to be satisfied.' He lifted the kettle and poured water into the teapot. 'I daresay she'll forget all about it.'

'You know that's not true.'

Kelvin looked at her after picking up the tray. 'Do you really mind whether she tells Luke or not? I mean, now that you know what kind of man he is you surely are not intending to remain married to him?'

'No. . . . Oh, Kelvin, I don't know! I can't think straight!' Her composure fled and she felt tears gathering in her eyes. 'You must remember that although I don't love my husband I do not hate him either. I married him of my own free will because I was drawn to him in some way—!'

'What way?' demanded Kelvin almost harshly.

She was reluctant to tell him the truth, naturally. 'I must have been drawn to him or otherwise I'd never have agreed to marry him,' she said after a pause.

'You admitted you married him to spite me—for revenge. I gathered that any man would have done at the time.'

A frown creased her forehead at that. 'Any man?' she repeated angrily. 'That's not true!'

Kelvin brought the tray into the living-room and set it down on the table. He straightened up and looked into her eyes. 'I repeat, any man would have done. I can understand just how you felt, so angry and humiliated that you'd have married any man who asked you. As it was you married the first man you met. It was crazy but, as I've said, I fully understand how you felt.'

'You think you understand,' she corrected.

Kelvin picked up the teapot. 'In what possible way could you have been drawn to a man like Luke Leoros?' he demanded. 'You didn't even know him!'

She had to smile. What would Kelvin say if she told him she had known Luke so well that she had almost surrendered herself to him even before marriage? 'It's something I do not want to talk about.' She sat down, crossing her slender legs, saw him look at them before his eyes travelled up to her face again. She took the tea he offered and helped herself to sugar. 'I don't think I want to do your typing, after all,' she said with a quivering sigh.

'I can't see why you are dithering like this, Martine. I should have thought that once you knew what kind of man your husband was you'd immediately have decided to leave him and ask for a divorce.'

'It's what you wanted?' Something within her sent out a warning light but she was unable to understand what it was all about.

'I want you back, darling.' He put down his cup and came to her. 'Martine, I am begging you to get rid of this man and marry me.' Distress caused his voice to falter and Martine looked at him with pity and yet accusation was there, too, in her lovely eyes, eyes still bright with the tears she had managed to hold back.

'It isn't so easy,' she quivered. 'Why did Sophia have to come between us! Why did we come here in the first place! There were a hundred sites in Greece we could have used.'

'I know. It was simple bad luck that we ever came here. Do you suppose I haven't thought so many times during these past weeks?'

'You were fully occupied with Sophia at first,' Martine could not help reminding him.

'Perhaps—yes, I agree,' he said on noticing her expression. 'I do agree, but do you know, Martine, that after only a short while I realised the affair would not continue? I was infatuated—and you must admit that Sophia's very lovely. I don't know what I'd have done if she had not thrown me over—whether or not I'd have thrown her over. All I do know is that there was a great deal lacking that had been there between you and me. It was different, somehow. There was no depth to it.' He took her hand and pulled her to her feet. His lips found hers and she stood passive, accepting but not giving . . . and yet all the time she was acutely aware of what had been, of the beauty of their courtship. How could she let it all go in favour of a marriage that was empty of love?

'The conflict within me is unbearable,' she confessed as she looked up into his face. 'I want love in my marriage, spiritual love. . . . Kelvin, what on earth must I do?' It was a cry from the heart, a desperate plea for advice which she knew would not be accepted without another ordeal of thinking, of decisions made and unmade, of near despair at her inability to make a calm resolve which she could keep.

'There's only one logical thing you can do,' he said reasonably. 'Tell Luke you've realised your mistake and you want a divorce.'

'He'd want to know the reason. I'd have to tell him what I know, of course—'

'Tell him?' Kelvin seemed disconcerted all at once.

'Surely you'd expect me to tell him what I know?' Martine looked at him in surprise, for it was plain by his expression that that was the last thing he had envisaged.

'No, I'd certainly not expect you to tell him what you know. For one thing, it would be indelicate—embarrassing for you both, and for another he'd very quickly tell you that what he did when he was single had nothing to do with you—and you must admit that it hadn't.'

She nodded, frowning heavily. 'I suppose you're right. . . .' She again had the impression that all was not open and above board in this matter, that there was some mystery, something which Kelvin was keeping from her. And yet what could it be? He had always been open with her, frank and scrupulously honest, so why should she doubt him now? 'I'll think about it,' she promised. 'Perhaps the best thing is to leave him right away.'

'Now—at once?' eagerly as he moved away, taking a couple of backward steps. 'I'm more than willing, love. We could move to another place—Mykonos, and do some work on Delos. You'd like that. You were so enthusiastic about it, weren't you?'

She merely nodded. Delos had been such a happy time, wandering hand in hand with her husband among the ancient ruins, the sacred temples, the sad fallen columns, seeing the lovely mosaics and wondering by what magic they had survived for so long, survived for modern man to come along and unearth them for his pleasure and gratification, helping him to form pictures of what life was like in those far off times when the Greeks brought civilisation to the Western world.

She looked at Kelvin and did not want to go to Delos with him. It was a memory she wanted to keep. . . . But why? Frowning, she made an effort to analyse her emotions, to find a reason for wanting to keep Delos as a memory that would bring back the happiness she had experienced in her husband's company. Sex had certainly not come into it—no, there was something else that day . . . something almost spiritual. . . .

The revelation hit her with blinding effect. She was in love with her husband. . . . A man who could never love her because of what another woman had done to him, a man cynical and hard where emotion was concerned, a man who ridiculed the possibility of love between a man and a woman.

'Well, darling, have you made up your mind?' Kelvin's voice came to her as from a distance.

'Yes,' she whispered in an agony of despair. 'Yes, Kelvin, I have made up my mind. I will ask Luke for a divorce. There is no future for me in a loveless marriage.' In a marriage where love is one-sided, she added, but to herself.

'You'll not come away with me at once?' Disappointment ran through his tone. 'It would be best, darling, believe me. I don't like to think of your having a scene with your husband.'

'I must tell him,' she said firmly. 'It wouldn't be fair to leave without a word of explanation.'

'A note would suffice.'

'Not for me. It would be shirking.'

'All right,' he agreed, but with a sigh of regret. 'I have to abide by your decision. When will he be back?'

'He said in a couple of days, or perhaps three, but he has a lot to do and might be away until the week-end.'

'And you'll be packed and ready to leave?'

She nodded, stinging tears at the backs of her eyes. 'Yes, Kelvin, I'll be packed and ready to leave.'

Chapter Seven

Luke phoned Martine that evening. She stiffened and closed her eyes, wishing she had not answered his call. 'Are you missing me?' he asked after greeting her. 'What are you doing with yourself?'

'Oh—er—pottering about.'

Her voice was stiff and cold and she heard her husband say, 'Something wrong, Martine? You don't sound too happy.'

'I'm all right. When shall you be back?'

'I rather think it won't be until Friday or even Saturday.'

'All right. I'll see you then.' She injected a note of finality into her voice and hoped he would say good night and ring off.

'There *is* something the matter,' he asserted. 'You had better tell me what it is.'

'When you come home, Luke.'

'Now!' on an imperious note which she strongly resented.

'It isn't anything we can discuss on the phone.'

'So it requires a discussion?' Plainly he was

puzzled but there was also a touch of anger in his voice as if he were impatient with her refusal to tell him what was wrong.

'It does, yes. I'm ringing off now, Luke, so I'll say good night.'

'Martine—wait—'

She replaced the receiver on its rest, her heart beating far too quickly. Anger rose within her at the knowledge that he could instill fear into her from all that distance.

'I don't know how I'm going to tell him,' she was saying to Kelvin later when they were having dinner in his living-room.

'Then come away with me tomorrow,' he urged, refilling her glass with the *Boutari*, a rich Burgundy type wine he had bought in the village along with the ready-made *stifado*—a meat and onion stew which he merely had to heat up in the oven.

'You can't leave when you're in the middle of your work here.'

'I've made copious notes; they could suffice.'

But Martine shook her head. Unpleasant though the confrontation with her husband might be, she would not dream of shirking it. Anyway, she owed it to him to be there when he came home, and to tell him to his face that she had changed her mind about the marriage and wanted to end it.

'He'll be back by the week-end,' she said. 'After that I can think of leaving.'

'You promised me you'd be packed and ready to leave,' Kelvin reminded her, moving the wine bottle to his own glass. 'You'll not go back on your word?'

'No, Kelvin, you've no need to worry about that.' It was ironical, she thought, that the reason for her decision to leave her husband was not owing to what he had done to Litsa—as Kelvin believed—but because of the revelation that had come to her, the knowledge that she was madly in love with her husband. It was the sure conviction that he would never love her which was the spur to her own action—or her proposed action—in leaving and asking for a divorce.

'But you won't come away tomorrow, and save yourself the unpleasant meeting with him?'

'I must do what my conscience tells me is right,' she returned, an unconscious note of apology in her tone.

He sighed deeply and changed the subject, telling her that he was disappointed by her reluctance to do his typing for him, at which she said she would do it; she would come early in the morning and make a good start.

'Thanks, darling. You've taken a load off my mind.'

After a dessert of a cream-filled pastry topped with almonds and honey they had coffee and cognac on the verandah, in the dark because Martine was afraid of being seen.

'Why afraid?' he wanted to know, going on to remind her that as she was leaving Luke anyway she had nothing to fear from the possibility of his learning that she had dined with the man she intended to marry, once her divorce was through.

'I'd rather not have him know I've been here,' was all she said. 'And I'd certainly not want him to know I am typing for you.'

But little did she guess that Luke was to know she was typing for Kelvin, and only a few hours after she had begun. At eleven o'clock the following morning Luke's car slid to a halt before the window of the room in which she was working. She glanced up and gasped, the colour draining from her face. Kelvin was out making a map of the Sanctuary, and for that at least Martine was thankful. But something akin to sheer terror caught at her nerves as she saw the murderous expression on her husband's face as he stalked into the room after having seen her clearly as he alighted from the car.

'I had an idea I'd find you here,' he almost snarled, moving across the floor with the lithe silence of a tiger. 'What does all this mean? Tell me at once!'

She stood up, then sat down again for her legs were like jelly beneath her. 'What—I thought—I mean, you said you'd be away until—'

'I came home because I realised something was wrong!' He glanced towards the door leading to the kitchen. 'Where's that fellow?'

'Kelvin? H–he's at the Sanctuary—working.'

'You didn't dine at home last evening,' he rasped. 'You were here—after I'd told you not to see him again—'

'Luke,' she broke in. 'I don't understand—how could you know I'd be here?'

'Because I've already been up to the house! I learned that you'd left early this morning, and also that you'd not dined at home last night!'

Her chin lifted and she assumed a reasonably calm exterior in spite of the fear within her. 'You haven't the right to dictate my actions!' she began, when he interrupted her to say, 'As your husband I have every right to expect you to keep away from other men!'

'Oh. . . . !' The colour ebbed from her face,

leaving it pale with an anger equal to his own.
'Just what are you insinuating?'

He set his teeth, eyes glaring, a sort of pagan
fury and ruthlessness in their depths.

'Get up from that chair,' he ordered. 'You're
coming home with me. I refuse to argue with
you here, in someone else's home!'

At first she knew an instinct to refuse but on
scrutinising his face more closely she had the
sense to do as she was told. 'I'll write him a
note,' she said quietly, wishing her nerves would
not act in this erratic manner. If only she could
be calm she felt she could cope with what was
before her, but the way she felt . . . **Why** did she
allow herself to be plunged into a state of fear
like this? Luke was only a man; he might have
the appearance of some Greek god but his pow-
ers were limited to what was mortal.

He stood while she wrote a quick note, then he
picked it up and read it. 'You can cross out the
last line,' he told her peremptorily, then threw
the piece of paper down beside the typewriter.
'You will *not* "be seeing him soon."'

She did as she was bid, thinking it did not
matter anyway. She could phone him from the
privacy of her bedroom.

Both she and Luke were silent on the short
drive up the steep, winding road leading to the
Villa Cladeos. But Martine was thoughtful and
decided that the best thing was to tell Luke of
her decision right away, taking him off guard
and making all his complaints unnecessary.

This she did, the moment he had unceremoni-
ously ushered her into the cool and flower-
scented living-room and closed the door, inter-
rupting his forceful and harshly-spoken, 'And
now, wife, you can begin your explanation—'

with, 'I might as well tell you at once, Luke, that I have decided to end our marriage.' She was very pale, and the perspiration was already visible in little beads of dampness on her forehead.

'You . . . have what?' The words came slowly, after a small pause during which Luke's face became almost evil and for the very first time the scar looked ugly—almost revolting. Martine shuddered and automatically stepped back, putting more distance between her husband and herself.

'I want more from marriage than sex,' she managed through dry and stiffened lips. 'Therefore, I want a divorce. I—I'm in love with Kelvin still—and he's in love with me. It's not sensible for us to—to be apart. . . . In spite of her resolve to face up to him bravely, Martine faltered, her nerves rioting, her heart thudding painfully against her ribs. For Luke wore an expression which reminded her of the fury of the very elements themselves—dark, and ominous as thunder.

'You've obviously been discussing this with Kelvin,' accused Luke through his teeth. 'And do you suppose the results of those discussions are anything to do with me?' His eyes were narrowed now, his mouth tight with the anger that consumed him.

'They are, Luke,' she answered with some difficulty. 'My sentiments are important—'

'You married me of your own choosing,' he broke in harshly. 'And that marriage stays—get that!'

She passed her tongue over her dry lips and stared at him, thinking that if she had seen him in a mood like this she would never have married him—never even have considered marriage. In fact, she would have run from him and hoped she would never set eyes on him again.

'You can't force me to stay with you,' she told him presently. 'I—er—I have my things ready to pack. I'd have had them packed if you'd not returned earlier than I expected. I promised Kelvin that I'd leave here with him immediately after I had told you that I wanted a divorce.'

The black eyes blazed for interminable moments then narrowed, while his face twisted and his fingers closed. Again Martine shivered, fascinated, held as prey is held, helpless, by a predator. Helpless? Her mouth went tight. She was not helpless! She was not going to allow herself to be terrorised like this!

'There'll be no divorce—'

'My mind's made up!' She snapped out the interruption, staring straight at him, defiance and challenge in her eyes. 'You can't do a thing about it—I am leaving you today!'

'By heaven you are not!' All the mastery and domination of the Greek god Zeus himself seemed to be ignited within him as, with a leap, he was across the room and she cried out a protest as he seized her wrist in a cruel and possessive grip.

'Luke, I—!' His fierce, attacking mouth stemmed the rest as it closed over hers, but with anger as the spur she set up a struggle which increased in strength when his possessive hand sought beneath the loose bodice she wore to close firmly and arrogantly on the curve of her breast.

'Leave me alone!' she cried wrathfully, gripping his wrist and digging her fingernails deliberately into it, actually hoping to draw blood. With a muttered oath he took her by the arms and shook her with ruthless abandon until she cried out for him to stop.

'Little wildcat!' He looked at his wrist and then at her. 'I'll beat you the next time!'

'There won't be a next time,' she quivered gaspingly while she endeavoured to get her breath back. 'I'm going!'

He took hold of her again and jerked her to him, finding her mouth in spite of her swift movements as she swung her head about, trying to beat him even while knowing that she would never succeed. He had her chin in a ruthless grip, forcing her head to be still, and then she felt his probing tongue, his roaming hands, his hard and masterful body compelling her to obey the demand of its pressure.

Tears pricked her eyes at her helplessness; she murmured a protest when at last he drew his mouth from hers. 'My—my mind's m–made up,' she said weakly, her whole body drained by his rough handling of her. 'I made a mistake in marrying you, but now I w–want to rectify it—!'

'What has happened during my absence?' he demanded, his anger evaporating as he stood there, towering above her, his dark scrutiny so probing that she felt he would read her very thoughts. 'You were all right before I went away,' he reminded her, his grip on her arms tight and masterful as she made an attempt to free herself. 'In fact, I had the impression that you would have liked to go with me.'

She could not deny it, and for a moment she considered telling him that she knew of what he had done to Litsa. But even if she did, that would not be an honest explanation of why she wanted to leave him. But to confess the truth was unthinkable; she could never confess to loving him, knowing he would never love her in return. She merely said, her voice still jerky with her breathlessness, 'The only thing that's happened is that I've decided to be with Kelvin—the—the man I l–love.'

His eyes seemed to probe even more deeply. 'Why the hesitation?' he wanted to know. 'Aren't you sure about loving Kelvin—?'

'Of course I'm sure!' she interposed swiftly. 'You know I love Kelvin!'

'After what he did to you?'

'A slip, but he's sorry. I know nothing of the kind will ever happen again.'

'You know no such thing.'

'I believe him—trust him.'

'Then you're a fool!' He paused, offering her the chance to say something. But she remained silent, looking at him, at the face which, freed entirely from the anger that marred it a few minutes previously, was the most handsome she had ever seen. The scar was no longer prominent and she thought it might one day be scarcely noticeable at all. Then she found herself dwelling on how he had come by it . . . in a fight with the brothers of the girl he had injured in a way which prevented her ever finding a husband, for in Greece no man is willing to marry a girl who has had another man. 'However,' Luke was saying, 'whether you believe him or not makes little difference. You and I are married and we remain married—understand?'

She bit her lip, feeling helpless again, caught in his mastery, conscious of his tremendous strength of character and its continued ascendency over hers. She was no match for him. . . . Vexed at the admission but forced to accept it, she knew that she was weak like this because of the magnetism which he exerted over her . . . as a lover. . . .

'You can't persecute me like this—' she began.

'Persecute?' The dark eyes glowered at her. 'Don't you dare use a word like that to me,' he gritted. 'You're my wife; I have treated you with affection and respect so there can be no excuse for your using that word.' His deep voice was quiet now, its accent scarcely noticeable, as was the scar, and once again Martine felt it would eventually disappear altogether. She stood looking up into his face, and suddenly she knew she could not leave him . . . not yet. His power, his compelling magnetism, were too strong for her to resist. It was all very well to make decisions when he was away from her, but what good were those decisions when, like now, he was close . . . and exerting his power over her senses? She swallowed hard, thinking of Kelvin, waiting there, having read her note, waiting for her to join him, complete with suitcases. It was laughable, really, the way both he and she had lightly decided to go away together without considering her husband's reaction, or in her case, her own weakness when under the influence of her husband's domination.

'Luke,' she began, 'I can't—'

'—stay with me?' The anger had dispersed again and there was only mockery and amusement in his gaze. 'But you *can* stay, my wife, and you will. Whatever reason you have for this wish to go to Kelvin, it certainly isn't anything to do with love.' He stared directly at her and she was compelled to lower her eyes under the arrogant conviction of his. 'I've said more than once that you and I need one another and you know it's true, don't you?' No answer from Martine and after a small pause he went on, 'Answer me, Martine.'

She bit her lip, angry at feeling so helpless, and at her own lack of resolve to do battle with him. For there was no doubt at all that she could leave him if she genuinely wanted to, if the determination was strong enough. But it had to be stronger than Luke's will and his mastery, and she felt that, for the present at least, it could not be that. She was still too strongly influenced by the physical pleasure he could give her, by his expertise and finesse, his experience which made him the perfect lover. Kelvin would never be the perfect lover; of this Martine had no illusions.

Luke was speaking again, and this time there was an imperative inflection in his voice which could not be ignored. 'I have asked you to answer me, Martine.'

She stared up into his dark implacable eyes and almost against her will the words came, low and meek and yet edged with anger and self-disgust. 'Yes, Luke, we—we n–need each other.'

The dark eyes had narrowed as he waited; they opened again and she hated the triumph in their depths. 'Just you remember that—always.'

'I shall have to see Kelvin and explain.' Her body felt drained; her mind had lost its clarity. 'I don't know what he's going to think.'

'His thinking should have come before his affair with Sophia,' came Luke's harsh rejoinder. 'We are all subject to actions which bring regrets, but we have to abide by the decisions we have made. At the time he was certain it was Sophia he wanted, so certain that he asked you to give him back his ring. That was final; you're now married to me and it stays that way, understand?'

She frowned and set her teeth. 'You have no need to repeat yourself,' she flashed. 'It stays that way. . . . ' For the present, she added, but silently. One day she would be forced to leave, simply because her love would drive her from a man who could never give her love in return. But for now she was his and she would continue to be his. And as she stared into his face she suddenly knew that this was what she wanted—to stay with him for the present, to enjoy his love-making, to be taken to the very heights of heaven, to experience rapture indescribable. She despised herself but, as on a previous occasion, she found a certain consolation in telling herself that she was merely following the primitive instinct of mating.

'Come here,' her husband commanded, and she wondered if, with his keen perception, he had guessed at her thoughts. She moved, slowly and reluctantly, drawn to him not only by the command but by some inexplicable power which she felt he must have inherited directly from the ancient gods—the pagan gods—of Greece. His arms came out and she was drawn into them, a suppliant without the wish or the courage to fight. His face moved close; she felt his cool, clean breath before her lips were taken, moistly, possessively, and she closed her eyes as she reciprocated, a drowning cataract of warmth flowing over her whole being, reaching her heart to infuse it with added heat. His arms were rough encircling her body, a brace of steel that ground her to his thighs, his hands roved deliberately as if he would bring it home to her that he was her master, with total rights over her. She relaxed against him, quivering involuntarily when his mouth found the pulse-beat in the delicate white hollow of her throat. His lips parted against it, a sensuously tantalising attack on her emotions and on any small resistance she might decide to make.

'It seems an age since we made love—' He paused and she heard the thick uneven sound of his breathing. 'I want you—now. . . .'

She did begin to struggle then, half-embarrassed, half-horrified at the idea of his taking her to bed at this time of day.

'No—I—you'll have to wait!'

A low laugh escaped him and he bent his head again to possess her lips. 'Unless you want me to pick you up and carry you to the bedroom, wife, you had best move willingly . . . and obediently. I have had enough this day to make me both impatient and angry.' He gestured towards the door. 'Off you go; I'll join you in five minutes' time.'

It was over an hour later when he said, his warm body naked and strong beside her, 'Well, my dear, are you fully convinced that you need me?'

With the aftermath of ecstasy quivering through every nerve and cell in her body, she heard herself say in pliant, husky tones, 'Yes, my husband, I am fully convinced.' And she turned to wind her arms about his hard and sinewed frame, her face close to his, her receptive nostrils keenly sensitive to the exciting male aroma of his skin. She saw his fine lips curve in triumph and mockery before they touched hers, touched them gently, while his hand covered hers as it lay on his stomach. A strange sigh rose from the depths of him and the silence was unfathomable.

'I shall go along and see this fellow, Kelvin,' he began when she interrupted him to plead, 'Let me do it, Luke. It will be hard for him to accept my change of mind; he's there now, thinking I'll be coming, expecting me at any moment to appear.'

Her husband laughed as he leant up on a supporting elbow. 'And here you are, in bed with me, having forgotten he ever existed.'

Instinct lifted her chin but she knew she lied when she said, 'I could not forget him, not when I'd made the promise!'

'Little liar.' Luke's mouth was on her throat, his warm hand cupping her breast. She sensed his desire to make love again and wondered at his strength. For herself, she was exhausted by the primitive violence of the storm through which they had both just passed.

She looked at the rays of the sun shafting through the drapes and murmured, shaking her head, 'It seems wrong to be in bed at this time of the day—unless one is ill, of course,' she added, feeling foolish because of the amusement on his face.

'How can such pleasure be wrong?' She made no answer and he added after a thoughtful pause, 'We ought to make love in the water—'

'Water!' she broke in with a gasp and a growing frown.

'Oh, not in the bath,' he laughed. 'I would find that a little cramped. No, in the sea, Martine, the warm soft sea when you feel you are wrapped in silk, when your partner's body slides and floats against yours, when everything comes without effort . . . !

His voice trailed off and she was impelled to ask, 'Have you ever made love in the sea before?'

He looked at her from above; he touched her shining hair and answered softly, 'Yes . . . but I very much doubt if the pleasure I derived was half as satisfying as it would be if you were my partner. We shall try it one day when we've been out swimming—' He broke off and kissed her hot cheeks. 'You're so beautiful when you're embarrassed, my Martine. You know, I'm an exceedingly fortunate man to have found someone like you.'

She thrilled to his words, half pretending he was in love with her. She touched the scar, a compulsive action born of tenderness, but then all the magic was blanked out by the knowledge of its origin. A brawl. . . . A fight during which he no doubt made his strength felt, but he had also gained a scar, and even as she looked it seemed to become livid, and a nerve within it began to pulsate. She withdrew her hand swiftly and saw his dark eyes narrow.

'You do not care for my disfigurement?'

It was the first time it had been referred to and for one impulsive moment Martine had the urge to ask him how he had received it. But within seconds she shrank from the idea and merely said, quite truthfully, 'It isn't normally noticeable to any degree. I think that one day it will disappear altogether.'

He nodded and automatically put a lean brown finger to it, tracing the line while a slight frown accompanied the gesture. 'The doctor assured me it would, but these things take time.' He paused in thought while Martine held her breath, half expecting him to give some explanation. But he merely withdrew his hand as she had done and, after kissing her lips and her throat and the pearly white swell of her breasts, he slid from the bed and took up a dressing-gown which he had previously laid across the end of the bed. Martine watched him put it on, colouring at the compulsion which made her look at him, naked and muscled, his skin brown as an Arab's, the small gold cross he wore gleaming among the raven black hairs on his chest. He turned his head after tying the cord and his strong profile gave way to his full face, noble and handsome, the features finely chiselled. Again she likened him to the statues of the Greek gods she had seen in the museums. A sigh escaped her. If ever he did come to love her it would be too good to be true—She cut her thoughts and shook her head. He would never love her; he had told her so on more than one occasion, had told her quite categorically that he did not believe in love between a man and a woman.

'What are you thinking?' His eyes moved from her face to the swell of her breasts, revealed even though she had drawn up the sheet and was holding it with one hand against her chest.

'It wasn't anything important,' she replied without looking at him. 'Er—if you will go I'll get dressed.'

'Go?' His brows lifted a fraction. 'Not shy all at once, surely?' he commented in tones of mocking amusement. 'Get up, wife, and let me enjoy what is mine.'

Anger surged and she drew the sheet right up to her chin. 'I want a little privacy—'

'Nonsense!' He had crossed the room in three long strides and before she realised what his intention was she found herself pulled from the bed and forced to stand, naked and beautiful, while her husband took his fill of the picture she made. A pulse rioted at one side of his throat; his other hand came forward to caress her hot cheek. Slowly he bent his head, and his kiss was gentle and reverent, the expression in his eyes distant and unfathomable. Martine had the strange sensation that he was doing battle within himself . . . fighting something . . . but what? She twisted and he allowed her to go, but stood there watching her every move and gesture as she put her clothes on, one by one, until at the end he took the dress from her and put it over her head, then turned her around so he could zip her up. They stood together, intimate and warm; she felt his hands come round to cover the softness of her breasts and every quivering nerve in her body craved for more. What was this pull, this complex magnetism that he could exert over her apparently without the slightest effort? He had only to touch her to set her emotions on fire with longing. Surely this was not a normal relationship . . . not healthy, perhaps. She turned in his arms and was kissed soundly, then slapped gently and told not be such a temptress.

Chapter Eight

Kelvin looked at her blankly and Martine averted her face and stared through the window of his sitting-room, absently noting the tangled shrubs and the wild fig tree lifting its branches above the trellis which was dripping with colour from bougainvillaea of various shades ranging from rose pink to magenta. The warm Grecian sun cast its golden light over the whole garden and the sky above was sapphire blue and cloudless.

'I don't understand.' Kelvin broke the silence at last, his voice accusing and angry and baffled all at one and the same time. 'You *can't* want to stay with him!'

She swallowed the saliva collecting on her tongue. 'I'm sorry, Kelvin, but—but—yes, I do want to stay with my husband.' She felt miserable at hurting him, this man whom she had so recently loved . . . or believed she had loved. She was now half convinced that Luke had been right all along and that she had never been in love with Kelvin. Nor had he been in love with her, Luke had asserted. Well, he had not been in love with Sophia either, it would seem.

'You promised—and it's only since talking to him that you've changed your mind!'

'We did talk, yes.'

Kelvin looked at her with suspicion in his eyes, and a shade of contempt, Martine noticed.

'It's the physical side of it.' Half question, half statement and to her chagrin Martine felt the colour mount her cheeks. A sneer caught Kelvin's underlip. 'They do say the Greeks are the world's greatest lovers—no, not the greatest,' he amended, flicking her a glance of scorn, 'the most amorous. So he gets you going, does he?'

'Don't be vulgar!' flashed Martine, her cheeks hotter than ever.

'I'm stating a fact. You never seemed that hot-blooded to me—but perhaps I, as a mere Englishman, do not have what it takes.' Turning his back on her he walked over to the drinks cabinet and lifted the lid.

She turned towards the door but was only halfway there when he said, 'Don't make a hasty decision, Martine, please. I love you and you love me. Sex won't keep a girl like you interested forever, not without something deeper to strengthen it.' He paused, bottle and glass held aloft. 'You're dishonest if you argue with what I am saying, darling. Give him up and come away with me as we arranged. Why, that scar is enough to tell you what sort of man he is! As I mentioned before, every time you look at it you're going to be reminded of how he came by it.'

She nodded even though she did not mean to. She could not verbally agree with him, though, but something in her expression caused him to add confidently, 'You don't deny anything, so in your heart you agree with all I have said.'

'The scar will fade—' She stopped, feeling foolish at the inanity of the remark.

'But the memory won't. Always there will be the knowledge of the damage he did to that girl.' Vehement the tone . . . but the eyes avoided hers and something quivered along Martine's spine.

She was profoundly conscious of the fact that, previously, she had sensed a mystery surrounding that scar. She heard herself say slowly, her eyes never leaving his face, 'Are you absolutely sure he received the scar in a brawl with Litsa's brothers?'

Kelvin seemed absorbed in pouring out his whisky. His eyes no longer avoided her scrutiny when he said at length, 'Of course I'm sure. In any case, you've spoken to Litsa so you know for certain that the little boy is his.'

She pursed her lips, still uneasy, still conscious of something that was not open and above board. 'Yes,' she said presently, 'I have spoken to Litsa. Nevertheless, I somehow cannot associate my husband with a dastardly act like that. He is a Greek and knows full well the harm he would be doing to that lovely girl. And she *is* lovely, Kelvin. You haven't ever met her, it would seem?'

He shook his head. 'No, I haven't.'

'Then you should.'

'Any particular reason?' he inquired with sudden interest.

'No . . .' Martine shrugged her shoulders, not knowing just why she had said what she had. 'It was just that I thought you should know what she is like.'

He frowned at her from above the glass he held. 'I have not the least desire to know what one of your husband's pillow friends is like.'

Martine set her teeth, and her eyes flashed fire. 'Don't talk about my husband like that!' she fumed. 'Nor should you talk about Litsa that way.'

'You appear to be strangely sympathetic towards Litsa.' He was puzzled yet still scornful in spite of the little interlude when he had begged Martine to reconsider and go away with him as they had previously arranged.

'She isn't bad just because she's had a baby out of wedlock!'

'In Greece she is.'

'I don't think so.'

'You agree with the affair then—the affair between your husband and this village girl?'

'Agree is an odd word for you to use, Kelvin.'

'Condone, then? Overlook?'

'I have to overlook it, seeing that it has already happened—and you have to remember that it happened a long while ago when Luke's affairs had nothing to do with me any more than mine had anything to do with him.'

'But you never had any affairs—or so I concluded.'

'By affairs I do not mean anything physical. I am speaking generally.' Martine suddenly realised that this was an inane conversation, getting them nowhere, and she edged further towards the door.

'Don't go yet.' He put down the glass and came across the room. 'Martine, you're out of your mind to throw away the happiness of two people —yours and mine, darling.' He had almost reached her but she frowned and warded him off

with outstretched hands, palms facing him. It
was an instinctive, protective kind of gesture
which had the desired effect of stopping him in
his tracks.

'I'm leaving, Kelvin—goodbye, and good luck.'

'You can't go like this!' It was a desperate,
pleading cry which seared her soft compassionate heart, and she did not remember, as many
would have done, that Kelvin had treated her
even more heartlessly than this.

'I must, dear Kelvin,' she said gently, touching
his sleeve in a tender little gesture. 'It's best for
us both—'

'How can it be best for us both?' he broke in
wildly. He was as a drowning man grasping at a
straw . . . but there was no straw there.

Martine was compelled to say, a little catch in
her voice caused by the tightness in her throat,
'There is more to my marriage than you think,
Kelvin. You see, although you are right in thinking that Luke does not love me, you are wrong in
thinking I do not love him.' She was pale and
knew it. But Kelvin was paler still; in fact, he
was grey about the mouth and cheeks, ashen
grey. The look in his eyes hurt Martine abomina-
bly, but now she did think of what *he* had done to
her, recalling the pain, the black misery of that
drive when all the time she was looking for the
headlights that would tell her that Kelvin had
come and that he was sorry and wanted nothing
more than to make up and be happy with her
again, just as if Sophia had never existed for
him.

'You—you're telling me the truth?' he managed at last, moving backwards and reaching for
the glass he had put down. 'You love him?'

She nodded slowly. 'Yes, Kelvin, I do. So you

see, it would never have worked for you and
me—'

'But I don't understand,' he broke in swiftly.
'Only a few hours ago your mind was made up;
you were coming away with me.' He shook his
head bewilderedly. 'You can't possibly have
fallen in love with him since leaving me.'

She smiled then, a wise and yet enigmatic
smile, rather like that of the Mona Lisa, thought
Kelvin, fascinated now as he awaited her reply.

'It doesn't take long for the fact that you're in
love to hit you,' she said gently. 'I knew it before
I left you this morning. I said I'd come away with
you for that reason, and not because of what I
had learned about him and Litsa.'

'For that reason?' He frowned at her in puzzlement.

'I felt I could not live with Luke once I realised
I was in love with him. You see, I know he can
never love me.' Her lip trembled and Kelvin's
frown went deeper into his forehead.

'So you were, in effect, going to use me,' he
gritted, ignoring her last sentence although she
felt sure it was in the forefront of his mind. What
a fool he must think her, loving a man who by
her own admission would never love her. 'My
word, Martine, I have had a narrow escape!
You'd have come to me, let me marry you, and
all the time you'd have been in love with another
man—'

'You need not stare at me with contempt like
that!' she could not help breaking in to say, her
eyes flashing with anger and indignation. 'You
seem to forget that this whole thing has come
about owing to your breaking off our engagement!'

'It would seem that it was a wise decision on my part! You have never loved me—never!'

'Perhaps not, but neither have you loved me—' She broke off and opened the door. 'There's no profit in this kind of quarrel so I'll say goodbye again. I hope you will accept this as final.' Her voice was cool because of the ache in her heart. If only Sophia had not appeared on the scene— She stopped her thoughts, for she realised that the girl's intrusion into their lives had actually been for the best. As both Luke and Kelvin said, she had never really loved Kelvin . . . nor had he loved her. They had found something attractive in each other, but that was not love. She supposed that, had they married, they would have been happy for a time, but eventually it would have dawned on one or both of them that there was a great deal missing and, like so many others, they would, sadly, have agreed to a divorce.

Martine could not bear to think of that, for in her subconscious there was the strong conviction that she and Luke would part one day since such a relationship as theirs had not sufficient strength to survive the normal hazards which appear even in the happiest of marriages. Deep dejection spread over her as she made her way back to the villa. Even her appreciation of the landscape was half-hearted—the painted fields of soft green and the darker green of olive groves, the banded gold and brown of the river bank, the blue of the flowing water, its ripples tinted with sunlight so that myriad diamonds danced upon its surface. Oleanders nodded, their perfume wafting across to her on the zephyr of a breeze, and higher up she saw the incredibly beautiful gardens of her husband's home—her home. But for how long?

It was inevitable that Luke should notice her dejection and a frown darkened his brow. 'What did he have to say?' he asked, having met her on the terrace where he had been giving instructions to one of the gardeners who had now moved some distance away.

'Nothing much,' she returned non-committally, but her husband was not to be put off so easily and he repeated his question as if she had not spoken at all. She glanced antagonistically at him and saw his mouth compress at her action. Resignedly, she said, 'He was upset and said I was a fool, that I ought to go away with him—At first he said that,' she amended, then wished she hadn't because she had obviously given Luke food for thought.

'At first? You mean, he changed his mind after awhile?'

'Yes, he realized I had never loved him.'

Her husband regarded her with an odd expression. He was above her, toweringly tall and self-possessed and infinitely superior. Martine wished she had half his self-confidence, wished her nerves would not throb so whenever she was being questioned like this by him. He looked so stern and forbidding and she wondered what kind of father he would make and whether he would terrorise his children.

'There must have been a good reason why he changed his mind so suddenly?'

'I can't remember—er—we were talking and I think he—he suddenly felt that what we'd had between us wasn't love after all.'

'I told you that,' abruptly and with a deepening

of his frown. 'You're keeping something back,' he accused and to her annoyance she felt the colour rise in her cheeks. 'What is it?'

She shook her head, for this was one question she had no intention of answering no matter how he coerced her. It would be unbearably humiliating to confess that she had fallen in love with him. He would ridicule her, laugh in her face while admonishing her, reminding her that he did not believe in love between a man and a woman.

'Is there any neccessity for this cross-examination, Luke?' she queried at length.

'I have a right to cross-examine my wife.'

'What a pompous, arrogant man you are!'

His eyes narrowed dangerously. 'Don't prevaricate,' he snapped. 'What exactly passed between you and Kelvin just now?'

'I've told you everything that passed between us.' It was her own secret which she was keeping back, and perhaps something in her expression convinced him that no matter how hard he tried there was something within her that she would never divulge to him.

But he was angry, and for the rest of the day this anger was evident. However, while they were having their coffee after dinner he said curiously, 'Did you talk with Socrates as you intended doing?'

She nodded, eyes brightening. 'Yes—yes, I did. Is he going to marry Thoula without a dowry?'

'He is, and that means you've effected a miracle. Perhaps this will eventually catch on in this area and dowries will become a thing of the past. You're a clever girl to have succeeded in breaking a custom, for custom dies much harder

than law where such old established ideas are
concerned.'

Her eyes still shone as she said, on a little note
of satisfaction not untinged with triumph, 'I'm
thrilled that Socrates has seen sense. It was so
absurd for him and Thoula to wait until they
were well into their thirties—as I know many
people here do—and for Thoula to then begin
raising a family. She doesn't want to be having
children when she's forty. . . .' Martine's voice
trailed away because of the sudden gleam of
amusement which had appeared in her husband's eyes.

'She will still be having children when she's
forty,' asserted Luke with a confidence that
grated on her mind and her ears. 'Greek wives
resign themselves to the fact that their main
function is to produce children—and it is boys
who are wanted, not girls.'

Martine's pleasure of a moment ago became
submerged by anger. 'Boys!' she scoffed. 'A fine
thing it would be if you men all had your wishes
fulfilled. Where would all your boys be then?'

He laughed at her anger, laughed as if he
could not help it. 'Don't get so up tight, my dear.
Nature will ensure that there are enough females to go round—'

'And this question of women bearing children
into their forties! It's high time they were edu-
cated!' She paused, but to her annoyance Luke
was still laughing, though mainly with his eyes
this time. She glanced away, determined not to
be affected by the attractiveness of him in this
mood. 'I sincerely hope you are not expecting me
to be having children when I'm forty!' She
stopped rather abruptly, colour infusing her
cheeks as embarrassment swept over her.

'If I decided that you should, my dear,' he remarked softly and with emphasis, 'then you'd have no choice. However, I am not desirous of having a vast army of children around me.' He paused to look into her eyes and suddenly there seemed to be a deep and dense emotion between them and the atmosphere was charged electrically.

Why should this be such an intimate moment? It was almost as if love, strong and secure, were passing from one to the other. . . . Strange sensations, impossible dreams . . . Martine's heart contracted and sadness filled her eyes, moistening her lashes.

Luke stared at her strangely before saying, in tones almost tender, 'How many children do you want, Martine?'

She shook her head and glanced away, still embarrassed. But presently she answered, almost able to see her children playing in these wonderful gardens . . . there'd be a swing and a climbing frame, a paddling pool . . . children's laughter . . . she could hear it echoing all around her, and she and her husband were watching the activity, pride in their eyes, love in their hearts. 'Three. . . . I'm an idealist.' She spoke what was in her mind regardless of the fact that her wild impossible thoughts had no bearing on what she and Luke were talking about. For the love she had pictured had been love for each other as well as love for their children.

'Three?' He lifted an eyebrow enquiringly. 'What kind?'

'Two girls and one boy.' She spoke challengingly and a smile touched the chiselled outline of his mouth.

'The males will be outnumbered—that is what you want?'

'I like little girls,' she said. 'They're as adorable as kittens.'

'All kittens grow into cats.'

'I agree that some girls grow into cats,' she said and knew at once that the subtlety of her words had come through to him.

'Sophia?'

'And her sister.' It was out before she could prevent it and for one anxious moment she awaited his reaction. But no frightening expression appeared on his face—just a nerve pulsating along the length of the scar, nothing else.

'You do not know Odette well enough to pass an opinion like that,' was all he said and changed the subject, saying that if she wanted three children then that suited him.

'And you don't mind having two girls?'

'What makes you so sure you can choose?' he said with a glimmer of amusement. 'We might have all boys—or all girls. However, I expect we shall be both happy and grateful so long as they are born perfect.'

She looked swiftly at him. How unpredictable he was! For at this moment he was so very human, his expression softened by the look in his eyes, the relaxed mouth which, though still sensuous, was compassionate too . . . and she longed for him to kiss her. . . .

He said softly, 'You're very tempting at this moment, Martine. I could spend the rest of the day making love to you.'

She coloured but the sharp retort which she was sure he felt was forthcoming never even entered her mind, much less left her lips. Instead, she turned away and announced her intention of going on to the Sanctuary for an hour or so.

'I'll come with you,' he said.

Was he afraid of her meeting Kelvin, or did he really have a desire to be with her in that sacred place where all was so peaceful and quiet—a legacy from those ancient times when not the least element of friction was allowed to intrude into the sanctity and inviolability of the holy precincts?

Luke added, watching her in some curiosity, 'What's wrong? Why the hesitation? Don't you want me with you?'

'Of course I want you,' she replied unhesitatingly. 'It will be nice to have company. And you can tell me all about it—the true history and the legendary.'

'I expect you read it all before you came.' He moved and she fell into step beside him, happier than she had been for some days.

'I did read about it, naturally, when I knew I was coming here. But the stories vary so much that it's difficult to get hold of the authentic one.'

'There's no authentic one; historians have not yet established the origin of the legend of Olympia. All that is known is that it began as a purely religious sanctuary, just as so many of our ancient sites did.' They had left the terrace and were walking slowly through the gardens, keeping to a path between a bank of cerise bougainvillaea on one side and a bed of roses on the other. When they left the garden proper the extensive grounds of the villa unrolled before them in ever-changing design and colour; the little stream, tributary of the Cladeos, cascaded over the stones in its bed, its waters glistening, brilliant and blue; the oleanders were pink and white and sweetly-perfumed. They bordered the bed of the stream, while beneath them wild poppies splashed colour, flaunting their bright crimson flowers against the emerald green of the undergrowth.

Luke spoke after a pause, explaining that the Sanctuary had originally been dedicated to the earth goddess, Gaea, wife of Uranos, god of the sky. 'Later power was seized by Kronos, after whom Mt. Kronion is named, and he and his wife, Rhea, were worshipped at Olympia, but even at that time we have no record of the Olympic legend.'

'The Games began much later, then?'

'Some historians credit Heracles with organizing the first Olympic Games. However, it would appear that the real revival was around 900 B.C. when a sacred truce was entered into by three kings, and Parliament had the power to punish offenders against that truce.'

'So it was because of this sacred truce that the Olympic Games really got under way?'

'That's right. The Greeks were always warring with one another, the various tribes engaging continuously in civil strife. But the Games brought this to an end periodically when heralds travelled through the country announcing the Games and that the truce had to be observed.'

'So everyone laid down their arms.' Martine shook her head. 'But it was only a temporary cessation of hostilities.' It was a statement, not a question, for Martine knew, of course, that once the Games came to an end fighting automatically began again. 'The Games didn't really do any good at all.'

'Oh, yes, they did, in a way,' argued Luke thoughtfully. He and Martine were in the wood-

ed lane leading down towards the site and as the
surface of the road became stony he reached
down to take hold of her hand. She felt her whole
body glow as the warmth of his grasp pen-
etrated. He glanced down at the precise moment
when she closed her eyes, as if in ecstasy at her
quivering emotions. His eyes were oddly wide
and questioning when she opened hers and met
his gaze.

Her smile was forced as she said, 'What good
did the Games do, then?' It was a question asked
only to end an uneasy silence on her part, for she
was baffled by her husband's manner and expression; she wondered a little fearfully if he
had made a guess as to her feelings for him.

'They brought the entire Hellenic race together, a fraternity bent on national unity
for the period of the Games.'

Martine shrugged her shoulders. 'It was such a
short truce, though,' she said, and as Luke made
no comment they strolled on in companionable
silence until they reached the gate leading to the
Sanctuary.

Luke paid the entrance fee and they went in.
There were only a few tourists so all was quiet
except for the occasional bit of chatter mingling
with the chirping of crickets and the sound of
sheep-bells drifting down from the hills. The
Sanctuary lay before them, the once flourishing
centre of art and culture and great athletic
achievement, a tranquil world where now only
the sacred ashes of a magnificent civilisation
remained, ashes in the form of ruined temples
and fallen columns. Yet something mysteriously
revealing in the atmosphere brought clear vi-
sions of the grace and glory of ancient Greece,
the country which brought civilisation to the

Western world. Martine, affected as always by the magic, captured by the beauty, experienced the gap of time between then and now . . . and yet she was reminded that in terms of geological time the centuries were as a mere snap of the fingers.

'I can picture it all,' she murmured, speaking softly because to speak more loudly seemed like sacrilege. 'The graceful competitors, nude and of perfect physique, competing in various forms of combat.'

'The foot and horse-racing, the discus and the javelin, the wrestling and the jumping. . . . ' Luke's voice trailed off meditatively and it seemed that he, too, was lost in the magic of those far off days which had somehow left unfathomable images behind to linger over the sacred precincts like some profound yet hauntingly intangible shadows of a past so great and glorious that even the ruthless forces of nature had not been able to erase them.

'I suppose,' commented Luke at last, 'that you've been all over this site many times?' His voice was cool all at once, and he seemed to frown within himself.

She said quietly, 'Kelvin and I have certainly done a good deal of work here.'

'It's all been done before,' shortly and with a sidelong glance which told her plainly that he was deriding Kelvin's work.

'Perhaps, but a travel book on Greece must include something about Olympia.'

'When is he expecting to finish?'

'I have no idea. I think he is almost finished here, though.'

'And where does he go then?'

'He wants to go next to Mykonos, in order to

visit Delos.' Martine had no wish to talk about Kelvin and she changed the subject as they reached the remains of the Temple of Zeus. 'The statue by Pheidias must have been marvellous. What a shame it was destroyed.'

'It was only one of thousands of treasures that were either lost or destroyed. Many found their way to Constantinople and the statue of Zeus was one of the most precious. It's a shame it did not survive.'

Martine was silent as they stood by the base of the Temple. She tried to picture that wonder of the world, the first of seven. Almost forty-two feet high even though the god was seated on his throne, it was done mostly in solid gold and ivory embellished with precious stones and ebony. The god's hair was of gold, and so were his cloak and sandals. Martine could not even begin to estimate the value in money; the aesthetic value was the saddest loss, though, and it was believed that the statue had been lost in a fire in Constantinople after it had been stolen and taken there by one of the plunderers who had descended on the Sanctuary as it began to decline.

'Nothing lasts,' murmured Martine and she thought about life and people—those who had gone before her and those who would come after. Everything must perish—even the earth itself one day in the distant future. A sigh escaped her and was noticed by Luke.

'What's wrong?' he demanded and she realized he had concluded that her thoughts were with Kelvin, with whom she had spent so much time here, among the precious ruins.

'I feel depressed at the knowledge that everything will one day disappear. Nothing, no miracle, can preserve the treasures man creates.'

'All is transitory,' he agreed in solemn tones.
'It pays us to grasp what pleasure we can, my
dear.' He sent her a measuring look. 'I believe I
have already advised you not to ask too much
but to take what is there, what is real and
tangible.'

'Because life is so short?'

'Yes, for that reason, Martine.'

'You mention pleasure—not happiness.' She
stared down at the massive base that had once
supported the columns which had long since
disappeared, toppled by earthquakes or broken
by wind and rain to become small pieces that
could be carried away by the overflowing rivers
or buried in the sediment left behind when the
waters had subsided. Some of the stonework
would have been carried off by villagers over the
centuries and would no doubt be found in someone's rockery or even forming part of a building.

'There is only a fine line between pleasure and
happiness,' began Luke when Martine interrupted him.

'No, I can't agree. Happiness covers time but
pleasure is fleeting.'

'Have it your own way,' he returned indiffer-
ently. 'I find my life pleasurable and am satisfied
with it that way. You, my wife, want more.'

'Love,' she said, though she had not meant to
say it aloud.

'Forget it,' he almost snapped, but strangely
turned from her just as if he would conceal his
expression. . . . Why?

Could he still be brooding on the loss of the girl
he had once been engaged to? Could he be
admitting that it was love—real love—he had
felt for Odette? But why, then, had he not taken
her back after her divorce? He had deliberately

married another woman just for spite—or perhaps because he had been determined to guard himself against the weakness of falling in love with Odette again. Yes, mused Martine, he would certainly consider it weakness if he had allowed himself to fall victim to the girl's charms a second time.

And that was why he had married someone else.

'Love is essential in marriage,' she could not help saying as they moved away, towards the path leading to the museum which was located not far from the archaeological site. 'I shouldn't have married you.'

'It was the best thing you ever did.'

'I always said you were pompous and self-opinionated!'

'And you are dishonest, mainly with yourself. You will only admit to needing me when you're in the ecstatic throes of passionate love-making.'

'Oh—what a thing to say!' Her protest only served to make him laugh. Martine would have derived considerable satisfaction from hitting him.

'Come, child, let us go and take a look at the museum.'

'You can't want to go there. You've seen the exhibits many times.'

But I am always happy to see them again.' He surprised her by tucking her arm into his as he quickened his pace a little. He glanced around, saw that there was no one in the immediate vicinity and bent his head and kissed her cheek. It was an unexpected action and one which Martine sensed was done on impulse. She smiled up at him and he responded; she searched his face but suddenly it became a mask, fixed, unreadable.

Complex man, with that unfathomable way of changing his manner!

A good deal of what was in the museum was Roman, but by common consent they made their way to the room housing the world-famous statue of Hermes by Praxiteles, done in the 4th century B.C.

'Hermes . . . messenger of the gods,' murmured Martine softly. 'Isn't he beautiful!' And yet, she thought, his body could not possibly excel that of her husband.

'It must be one of the most beautiful statues ever executed,' agreed Luke. 'You know of course who the baby is?'

She nodded. Hermes was carrying the infant Dionysos, the god of wine, to be cared for by the nymphs of Boiotia.

'The baby was the illegitimate son of Zeus and Semele, and as Zeus was afraid his wife would have the child killed he told Hermes to carry it off to the nymphs.' She was half laughing as she finished, and she shook her head. 'You know, Luke, it always seems *true* to me.'

'Yet it's all fairytales.'

'I know, but as you once said, it was all real to the ancients.'

'Paganism.' He seemed a long way off, remote as the people about whom they were talking. Martine glanced upwards, noting the classical lines and curves of his face, the straight nose of the ancient Greeks, both men and gods, the mouth with its full, sensuous lips, the deep-set eyes beneath a stern dark brow. 'Yet, today, most Greeks are devout, and in the villages few of them would miss church on a Sunday.'

'But they kiss the ikons; that's a form of paganism still.' She was glad her husband did not have ikons about the house. Most Greeks did, and some—mainly women—would light candles every night and leave them there, lighting up the faces of the saints. Yes, saints now, not gods carved in stone. What was the difference? Paintings on canvas, carvings in stone . . . all to be revered, worshipped. . . . Dejection spread through Martine again and she shivered.

I wish I could be happy, she thought silently. This dejection will pull me right down in the end.

Chapter Nine

A sky of translucent silver and a softly-gliding
moon, the quivering lustre of amethyst and
pearl on the hillsides, the drowsy gardens with
their pools of black onyx beneath clumps of trees
or flowering bushes all lent their beauty to the
villa. Unreal as the perfumed breeze sweeping
in from the north, soft as velvet on your face,
unreal yet beautiful beyond description, they
stood.

Martine stood on the verandah of her bedroom, her long flowing dress clinging to her
shapely legs, its folds captured by the breeze.
She lifted her face to the light and the gentle
rush of air; she breathed deeply and wondered
why she could be unhappy in such magical
surroundings. She had everything . . . almost.
There was the house, elegant and showing every
sign of wealth and good taste; there wasn't a
thing she wanted to change. There was the
glorious setting, the servants and there was her
handsome husband. . . .

'Dreaming, my dear?' His voice behind her was edged with sardonic amusement; his hands on her throat were as warm and gentle as the lips that caressed her naked shoulder. She quivered and turned, reaching up to press her hands against his shoulders. She felt his muscles ripple, knew his instant need as he brought her slender body close so that she would feel the granite hardness of his thighs. He could hurt, and she thrilled to the pleasure-pain, just as she did when his lips became merciless, as they often did, or his possessive fingers found the places that were the most sensitive and the most delicate. Yet on the whole he was gentle with her; it was only when carried to the primordial stages that he forgot his own strength and she had to cry out to make him remember that she was soft and feminine and vulnerable.

'You're the loveliest thing I have ever owned. . . .' His breath was cool and fresh against her softly-parted lips, his hand on her hair light as the caress of a summer breeze. 'It was a fortunate moment in my life when I stopped up there on that hilly road to offer you assistance.'

'I thought you were Kelvin and threw myself into your arms.'

'I was stunned—'

'—but not for long! And then it was I who was stunned.'

'Obviously Kelvin kisses differently.'

'Gentler!'

'But not as satisfying.'

She laughed against the smooth linen of his evening jacket, then lifted her face, offering her lips, tempting him, flirting with him, but just when he was about to accept the invitation she said saucily, 'It's time we were going down for dinner.'

'Wretch!' She was slapped, then kissed soundly and not released until she began fighting for breath. 'Let that be a lesson to you, my girl!' He lifted her and carried her into the bedroom then set her on her feet. 'I suppose,' he remarked dryly, 'that you've transferred your lip rouge to me.'

'A little,' she laughed and produced a tissue from the box on the dressing-table. She offered it to him but he made her dab his lips herself. 'Are mine smudged? Really, Luke, you ought not to kiss me at this time of the day!'

'I shall kiss you whenever I like,' was his smooth rejoinder as he nodded his head in answer to her question. 'Yes, it's smudged.'

Dinner was somehow different that evening, more intimate, but perhaps it was because of the candles and the flowers and the sparkling champagne that Luke had decided to have with the meal. Martine was not really up to the quality wines her husband had in his cellar and after a glass and a half she was soaring on a cloud. But she realised Luke was behaving differently, not so coolly impersonal before the servants, not quite so reserved when speaking to her in their presence. He smiled a little more often, too, and listened to her more interestedly when she was telling him something.

Perhaps, she thought much later as she walked with him in the garden, he might one day come to love her. . . . But no—it was impossible!

The following day Martine came upon Sophia when she was in the village doing some shopping. Sophia's attitude was without doubt hostile and so Martine was instantly on her guard.

'I thought you'd have decided to go back to Kelvin before now.' There was a dark and antagonistic expression on the younger girl's face, marring its exquisite beauty.

'I happen to be married, Sophia,' returned Martine crisply, 'and, therefore, my place is with my husband.'

'But you're in love with Kelvin.'

Martine's eyes opened wide. 'Am I? You apparently know more than I do, Sophia.'

There was an audible gritting of teeth before Sophia said, 'Sarcasm's the lowest form of wit!' Her tone was sharp, her words more noticeably accented than usual.

'Don't be trite!' Martine's expression held contempt and the other girl began to colour up. Martine paused a moment in indecision, but eventually she said curiously, 'What did Kelvin say to make you change your mind about telling Luke of what you saw?'

'Kelvin didn't tell you himself?' Sophia's voice was equally as curious as Martine's had been.

'No—and I feel there is some mystery, Sophia.' Another pause before Martine added, glancing along the street, 'Perhaps you'd join me for coffee and tell me all about it?'

'About what?' Sophia looked away as she spoke. 'I don't know what you mean about a mystery.'

'I think you do,' with a sort of gentle persuasion. 'What about that coffee?'

Sophia looked at her, a hint of defiance mingling with the hostility which was still there in her manner. But she said at last, 'All right, I'll have some refreshment with you—but as for there being anything to tell—'

'Let us go along to the *cafeneion,* then,' suggested Martine and moved on in the direction of the little pavement cafe where the usual scene was being enacted—dark-skinned men lounging at the tables, legs sprawled and open—Martine had always thought that every move and posture of Greek men portrayed their interest in sex—while their hands were occupied either in playing *tavli* or clicking their brightly-coloured strings of worry beads. The waiter was busy serving *ouzo* and *mezes* or tiny cups of the black and syrupy Turkish coffee. One or two tourists were sitting, watching all that was going on with interest.

Martine and Sophia were fortunate in finding a seat away at one end and they gave their order. Sophia had a glass of wine while Martine had her usual light coffee served in a large cup.

'You had every intention of telling my husband of what you had seen,' began Martine without preamble once the waiter had gone. 'Why did you change your mind after Kelvin had spoken to you?'

'Ask Kelvin what he said.'

'So you really are adamant? You're not going to tell me anything?' Martine's hopes of getting something out of the girl were dying and she wondered what had made her so optimistic in the first place.

'You don't seem afraid of what your husband would say if I did tell him,' said Sophia curiously, completely ignoring what Martine had just said. 'I should be terrified in your place. Luke can be a savage when his temper's roused.'

'You've seen him in a temper?'

'My sister has—' Sophia broke off and shuddered.

'She jilted him. It was only to be expected he would be angry.'

'He was more than angry.' Another curious glance as Sophia said, 'If I were to tell him of that little love scene between you and Kelvin he'd probably wring your neck.'

Martine had to laugh, much to the other girl's surprise. 'He'd not do that, Sophia. He likes being married to me no matter what you might think to the contrary.'

'He doesn't love you. He loves my sister.'

Silence. Martine had no truthful answer to give to that, so she said after awhile, 'Greeks do not normally favour divorce, and so Luke and I are not likely to have one, if that is what your sister is hoping for.' This was not actually a truthful comment but Martine had no intention of allowing either Sophia or her sister to cherish the hope that Luke would one day be free to marry Odette.

'My sister had a divorce.'

'Luke has different ideas from your sister about marriage.'

'Why haven't you gone back to Kelvin?'

Martine shot her a glance, taken aback by the abrupt change of subject. 'I never had any intention of—'

'Oh, yes, you did,' broke in Sophia rudely. 'He told me—I think he was being spiteful, not that I cared! I've found someone else. Kelvin said you'd given him your promise that you'd leave Loukas and go away with him. Something made you change your mind and I can tell you now,

Martine, that I have every intention of —er—
spilling the beans—Is that what you call it?'

Nerves tensed, Martine said, 'You were only
willing to keep quiet if you knew I would leave
my husband?' The mystery was unfolding even
though Sophia had had no intention of its doing
so—not all of the mystery but at least some of it.
Martine felt that the most important, the most
vital, clue was still going to be withheld from
her.

Sophia shrugged and said casually, 'I felt that
so long as you were leaving there was no need to
divulge to Loukas what I knew.'

'You meant us to part.' It was a statement and
a small pause followed as Martine fully assimi-
lated what she had just heard. She glanced at
Sophia, who was idly watching a heavily-laden
donkey ambling along the street, a shaggy dog
on one side of it and a farmer clad in baggy black
pants on the other. He had a switch in his hand
with which he tapped the animal's flanks now
and then but the donkey still ambled along at its
own chosen pace.

'Loukas belongs to my sister.' Sophia spoke at
last, turning her attention to Martine. 'And you
belong to Kelvin, so the sooner you see sense the
better. I shall give you a couple of days to make
up your mind and then, if you haven't left and
gone away with Kelvin, I shall tell your husband
what I know.'

'I am not afraid,' returned Martine, marvelling at her control. Inwardly she was quaking at
the idea of a confrontation with her husband
after Sophia had divulged what she knew; described with embellishments in plenty what she
had seen.

'Loukas will kill you!'

'Don't be melodramatic,' admonished Martine, who felt she was speaking to a child even though Luke had told her the girl's age was nineteen. 'You can tell Luke everything if you must, but it will be totally ineffective; there will be no divorce for my husband and me.'

'If only I hadn't taken Kelvin from you this would never have happened!' snapped Sophia, obviously more furious with herself than anyone else.

'But you did take him from me,' returned Martine gently, 'and so the damage is done.'

'You're so calm!' It was a complaint, spoken in tones that could only be described as peevish. 'Aren't you afraid of Loukas?'

Martine said nothing; she was glad when the waiter appeared with the tray, his broad smile revealing the inevitable gold fillings, while his dark and roving eyes instinctively went first to the curves of Martine's breasts and then to the rather more exposed curves of Sophia's.

'Eet will be sixty-five drachmae,' he said in very broken English, and held out his hand.

'Later,' said Sophia shortly, speaking in Greek. 'Go away!'

'I'll pay,' from Martine who always treated those who served her with respect. 'Keep the change.' She gave him a hundred drachmae.

'*Efkharisto poli!*'

'You shouldn't tip them,' snapped Sophia. 'They come to expect it all the time.'

'What I do is my own business,' returned Martine levelly. 'Don't make any comments like that again, Sophia.'

The younger girl's mouth compressed. 'You

speak to me as if I'm a child!' The hostile fury in her voice matched to perfection the set of her mouth and the glitter in her eyes. Martine wondered as she drank her coffee just what Kelvin had seen in the girl. True, she was lovely to look at, but underneath she was poison.

'I merely asked you to refrain from commenting on my actions.' Martine's attention was arrested suddenly by the couple who had just disappeared round a bend in the road. Kelvin and Odette. . . .

Sophia had also seen them and her eyes became veiled even as she sent her companion a covert glance. Martine said nothing and neither did Sophia, and it was not long before the two said goodbye after leaving the *cafeneion*.

Martine sat thoughtfully on the verandah, pondering the situation in the light of what Sophia had threatened to do. At last she rose and went in search of her husband, whom she knew would be in his study at this time of the afternoon. She knocked quietly and entered after she heard his 'Come in.' He glanced up from some papers he was perusing and leant back in his chair, a half smile on his lips.

She looked at him from her place by the door, which she had closed behind her, and, as always, she found herself affected by his strong masculine appeal which was manifest even in the arrogance and superiority which were almost always present, a legacy from his ancestors.

'What is it?' he inquired when she did not speak. 'You look rather anxious. Something wrong?'

She shook her head, an automatic gesture which was belied by her words, 'There is—yes, Luke.' She glanced at the chair facing him on the opposite side of the big oak desk at which he was seated.

He said quietly, 'Sit down, Martine, and tell me what is wrong. It must be urgent for you to come here to me at this time.'

'No, it's not all that urgent.' She spoke slowly, trepidation thickening her voice. 'It is rather important, though.' She sat down, nerves taut, heart racing madly. Anger surged because of her fear; it always was that way—fear made her angry, had done so ever since she could remember.

Her husband looked at her and suddenly she suspected that he was ready for her to broach the subject of Kelvin, saying she wanted to go to him after all.

'Well?' he murmured, eyes glinting as he leant a little further back in the chair as if wanting to feel the upholstery at his spine, 'Let us not waste time, Martine.'

She was a long time in speaking, for the whole room seemed to reflect the autocratic manner he adopted; he seemed ready to pounce on her, to inflict his will in ruthless domination. But at last she managed to say, her voice surprisingly steady considering the tumult within, 'It's about something that happened when you were away in Athens.' She paused a moment but her husband did not speak. His scrutiny was keen, though, his eyes narrowed. 'I'd gone to see Kelvin—you knew that, of course.'

'Of course,' softly and with a question in the depths of his tone.

'I—we—that is—Kelvin and I were—were affected emotionally and—and . . .' She tailed off, almost flinching under the unmasked evil of his stare.

'You're telling me you were—unfaithful—?'

'Good heavens, no!' The idea that her hesitant words would give that impression had not for one second entered Martine's head. The vehemence and swiftness of her denial had their affect. Luke, who had become tensed and upright, relaxed his body again and his face lost most of its savagery. Heaven help me if *that* was what I had come here to confess! Martine thought.

'What, then?' after a pause. 'You were saying that there was an emotional scene between you and Kelvin.'

She nodded, her mouth dry, like sawdust. 'We were embracing and—and kissing when—when Sophia arrived. She threatened to tell you what she had seen.'

Luke, though grim, was puzzled, too, and there was evidence of this in his expression as he asked, 'Why hasn't she told me, then?'

'Kelvin persuaded her not to. You see—' She stopped a moment and stared at her hands, resting tensely on the pleats of her skirt. 'You see,' she began again, 'Kelvin believed I'd go away with him, and so he convinced Sophia that there was no need for her to go running to you with her tales.'

Luke frowned at her. 'Why have you told me this?' he demanded. 'Surely there was no need to do so?'

'Sophia's now given me two days in which to make up my mind. If I don't go away with Kelvin then she's going to tell you of what we—we were doing.' Martine's voice quivered and her eyes were wide and scared. She noticed the ruthless lines of his face, the gleam of anger in his eyes and waited breathlessly for his fury to descend upon her. To her amazement he rose and, coming to her, pulled her gently to her feet. No rough handling, no wrath to make her shrink away, nerves rioting.

'Sophia's threatened you, frightened you.' Luke's teeth gritted and the glitter in his eye was like an ember fanned to life. 'The little cat! Why didn't you come sooner? Why allow a wretch like that to put fear into you?'

Martine could only stare, first into his face and then at the hand that held hers, gently . . . almost protectively. How unpredictable he was, taking her part when she had fully expected some form of punishment as a reward for her confession.

'Aren't you angry?' A stupid, superfluous question. But Martine was still so taken aback that she could think of nothing else to say.

'Angry, yes—with Sophia! What I should like to know,' he said, again frowning in puzzlement, 'is what she hopes to gain?'

'She hopes that I will go away with Kelvin.'

Luke's frown deepened. 'And what benefit would that be to her?'

Martine paused a long time, her eyes on his hand, holding hers, his thumb moving absently over her knuckles. 'I believe she—she would like you and Odette to—to get together again.' There, it was out. Not what she had intended saying, but she was glad now, for Luke knew everything. . . .

Everything? No, for she herself did not know everything. She felt sure there was still a mystery, some circumstance which was being kept from her, both by Kelvin and Sophia.

Luke had thrown back his head and his laugh rang out in the silence of the room. 'What a hope! Surely you told her there was no chance?'

Martine nodded her head. 'I told her you'd never divorce me.'

Luke's gaze became curious. 'You could be so sure?'

Again she nodded, saying yes, she *could* be sure. 'I know you like being married to me,' she added, her voice rather strained because her own love was not returned.

'And so I am to expect a visit from our young friend, Sophia.' Luke had made no comment on what Martine had said but she did wonder at the way he suddenly dropped his lashes . . . hiding his expression?

'If I haven't gone in two days, yes.'

'It will be interesting.' There was both contempt and humour in Luke's tone. 'Young Sophia will get more than she bargains for.'

Martine stared down at his hand again and, noticing, he drew her gently to him, tilted her face and kissed her lips.

'I can't understand your attitude,' she said and her husband laughed in the most attractive way, causing her heart to contract and then flutter as her anxiety was released.

'You expected me to be angry, I suppose?'

'It was a very natural conclusion.'

'I rather think you have suffered enough already.'

'I certainly was—er—apprehensive.'

Again he laughed. 'That's mild. You were scared out of your wits.' A pause and a glimmer of amusement in his eyes as he saw hers flash. 'I must say it's gratifying to know that my wife is aware of the mastery of her husband.'

He was asking for it, she knew, but instead of losing her temper and thereby adding drama to the situation, she smiled saucily and said, peeping up at him provocatively, 'And it is nice for a wife to know that she can soothe the lion in his den without much trouble at all!'

'Don't be too confident. I just happen to be in a mellow mood!'

'A most attractive mood—' She hadn't meant that to be spoken aloud but it was there before she could hold it back.

'Thank you, my dear,' he said gravely. 'I'm flattered.'

She coloured, not too sure if he was being faintly sarcastic with her. But whatever, he drew her to him again, closely and tenderly, looking deeply into her eyes before bending his dark head to take possession of her lips. She lifted her arms to put them around his neck, aware of a lightness within her, a surge of pleasure which brought a sparkle to her eyes. Luke stared down into her lovely face, his fingers combing through the bright mass of her hair.

'How beautiful you are. . . .' The words vibrated with a passion that was gentle, his breath cool and clean as a morning breeze. She thrilled to his nearness, to the intimacy of the moment, thinking of her fear when she had decided to make her confession. Fear that had proved to be groundless because her husband had been kind and understanding, had overlooked a good deal because he had the sense to realise that there must have been an intimate scene between her and Kelvin, or otherwise they would not have been contemplating going away together. 'I ought to stop everything and make love to you.'

She looked up, laughter in her eyes, laughter which she hoped would hide her love. 'It's not the right time,' she retorted teasingly. 'Night time is for lovers.'

'You're coming out of your shell, my dear,' he declared unexpectedly. 'Not so long ago you would have blushed and refused to make any comment.'

It was true. But this interlude was so intimate, so different from any other that had taken place between them, that she felt close and secure and able to speak her thoughts aloud.

'I suppose I had better go,' she said reluctantly as she drew away from him. 'You're busy by the look of things.'

'So you are not in the mood for love?' His voice teased but his expression was serious. Martine, a little embarrassed now, backed towards the door. 'Very well, my dear—' He glanced at his watch. 'I think I might finish early and take you for a walk.'

Her eyes shone up at him across the space separating them. 'I'd like that, Luke,' she said eagerly, and he stared for a long moment, as if he were thinking about saying something, but after awhile he shrugged lightly and said he would be with her in about an hour's time. She hesitated, conscious of feathery ripples along her spine, profoundly aware that there was something tense and unfathomable in the atmosphere. While she watched, Luke returned to the other side of the desk and sat down. Martine turned and quietly left the room.

Chapter Ten

The following day Martine ran into Kelvin, both having gone into town to do some shopping. He greeted her as if they were still friends, albeit a little coolly and so she matched her mood to his.

'Hello, Kelvin. How is the book progressing?'

'As well as can be expected under the circumstances.' He fell into step beside her as she went along the street towards the chemists where she was to buy a few toilet requisites for herself and some after-shave for Luke. 'Has Sophia spoken to you lately?' he asked after a moment of hesitancy.

'She has, and she threatened to go and see Luke.'

'To tell him what she had seen?'

'What else?' tartly and with no intention of admitting that she had already put her husband in possession of the facts. 'She's bent on destroying my marriage—'

'She feels that Luke belongs to Odette.'

'And you?' sharply and with a curious look for

169

there had been something strange in Kelvin's tone of voice, some undercurrent which was as disturbing as it was incomprehensible.

Kelvin drew his brows together in a heavy frown which only added to Martine's puzzlement. 'Why should I have any particular opinion on the matter?' he asked and Martine knew for sure that he was prevaricating.

'I saw you with her yesterday. I was with Sophia—we met and I suggested she join me in a cup of coffee. I had hopes of getting something out of her because I feel there is a mystery— something you are all keeping from me.'

'All?'

'You and Sophia, and possbily Odette as well—' She stopped abruptly as, sending him an upward glance, she saw his lashes sweep down to hide his expression. Her nerves tensed; she was definitely sure now that the three had some scheme in common . . . and it was aimed destructively in her direction. . . .

'You say you saw me with Odette?' Casual the tone but she could tell that it was forced. 'We met by chance and it was natural that we'd walk together.' He paused a moment. 'You'll be in serious trouble with your husband when Sophia tells him what she saw.'

A look of contempt was Martine's only reaction for a space, but eventually she said, the look in her eyes reflecting what was on her lips, 'You're really spiteful, aren't you, Kelvin? You always seem to forget that this whole situation was brought about by your fickleness.'

'All right,' he snapped. 'There's no need to keep on reminding me!'

'Then don't you try to frighten me!'

He glanced down into her lovely face. 'You don't appear to be afraid, and that puzzles me because from what I've heard of your husband's temper he'll most likely beat you.'

'You'd like to think he would?' She wondered what his reaction would be were she to tell him just how her husband had taken it when she made her confession. But Martine had no intention of telling him and by so doing have him tell Sophia. No, Martine was human enough—and catty enough!—to want Sophia to confront Luke and get what was coming to her!

'This lack of fear puzzles me,' said Kelvin again and Martine actually laughed because his words were in the nature of a complaint, pettishly spoken.

'I am not afraid of my husband, Kelvin,' she said after a pause.

'Then you're a brave woman.'

She made no comment on that for, as had been the case on several previous occasions, she felt the conversation with Kelvin was inane, pointless and ruffling to them both. However, she agreed to sit at the outdoor *cafeneion* when he invited her to join him for a cool drink. They sat under a canopy of vines where lush green grapes were hanging. On the air came the scent of oleanders and roses, drifting from the side garden of Marco's whitewashed, flat-roofed villa. Beyond the flowers was the *perivoli,* the orchard where he grew citrus fruits—oranges and lemons and bright green limes.

They had just had their drinks placed before them when Martine spotted Litsa, walking slowly, a basket of groceries in her hand. She looked, and caught Martine's gaze. Martine,

acting on impulse, lifted a hand swiftly to
beckon the girl over. There was a slight hesitation after Litsa stopped and then she smiled
and came on. But there was something strange
about her—furtive—and her eyes strayed cov-
ertly towards Kelvin. Martine had the firm conviction that the girl knew who he was even
though she had never met him. She introduced
them and her deductions were strengthened.
Yes, Litsa's lack of surprise proved beyond
doubt that she had guessed who Kelvin was.
As for Kelvin himself—well, thought Martine
with a little shock of surprise, his gaze was
one of deep admiration to say the least. She
recalled his saying that in Greece a girl who
has a child out of wedlock is considered bad.

'Do sit down.' Kelvin seemed to come to after
his long and fixed appraisal and he rose to his
feet, offering Litsa his chair. 'What can I get you
to drink?'

A smile fluttered. She was shy, hesitant and
unsure of herself and Martine suspected she was
sorry she had come over to join them. But she
answered presently, 'I would very much like to
have of the cold lemonade—if you please.'

Kelvin clapped his hands in the way the
Greeks did to bring the waiter over. 'Another
chair and a glass of iced lemonade,' he ordered
and within a couple of minutes both had arrived. Kelvin seemed more than eager to put the
Greek girl at her ease; he chatted with her while
Martine was left to listen, fascinated by the way
the two were getting along together. They might
have known one another for months, she mused
when at last she rose and said she must go. This
caused Litsa to look scared and rise also.

'I must go too,' she murmured but it was plain

by the way she looked at Kelvin that she did not really want to go.

But she was vitally conscious of the conventions, knowing that her reputation was already besmirched and, therefore, she dared not risk being seen alone with the Englishman. Martine frowned as all this was borne in on her. She looked at Kelvin, a look that spoke volumes. And she saw that his expression spoke volumes, too!

It was only a week later that Martine said to her husband, 'I have an idea that Kelvin has found someone else.' She stopped, then watched Luke's face closely as she added, 'He seems to have become exceedingly interested in a girl from the village called . . . called Litsa—'

'Litsa!' he broke in sharply. 'Litsa Katsellis?'

'The one with the little boy.'

Luke's glance was sharp and narrowed, ice suddenly in his manner. Martine regretted the impulse by which she had been urged to mention Litsa and the situation fast developing between her and Kelvin.

'You're telling me that Kelvin's fallen in love with Litsa? He knows of course that she's never been married?'

Martine felt herself going cold inside, for she could scarcely believe that Luke could be so indifferent, callous almost, as he discussed the girl he had so heartlessly wronged. Her eyes registered contempt and her mouth went tight. But there was nothing unusual in her voice as she said yes, it did seem that Kelvin was falling in love with Litsa.

'You sound as if you know the girl.' Luke's scrutiny was long and interrogating.

'I have met her, yes.'

'How do you know that Kelvin's interested in her?' he demanded as if the question had just come to mind.

'I was with Kelvin in Marco's *cafeneion* when Litsa joined us—'

'You were with Kelvin—on view to everyone in the town!' Cold fury edged his voice as he added through his teeth, 'How dare you keep on seeing him when I've warned you so many times? I forgave you the lapse you confessed to, and I sent Sophia on her way with reddened cheeks when she came here with her tale-carrying, but at least I believed you and Kelvin had finished seeing one another!' He was wildly angry; Martine, pale but composed, waited until he had stopped speaking before reminding him that, as Kelvin was seriously interested in Litsa, he was being absurd by adopting this attitude. And then she stopped, her heart giving a little lurch, for it had just occurred to her that Luke's whole manner was that of a jealous husband. . . .

They had been standing on the verandah of the living-room, and she stepped close to the wrought iron balustrade to lean against it for support as she tried to gather her wits, to bring order to the turmoil in her mind. For this suspicion could not possibly have any foundation, she was telling herself one moment, yet the next she was saying she must believe the evidence of her previous observation. She turned to look directly at her husband and saw that he had been slightly taken aback by the logic of her remark. And as the silent moments passed he seemed to be discarding his anger altogether. His face lost its harshness and his mouth relaxed, the lower lip taking on that fullness, that distinctly sensuous aspect which, oddly enough, only added, enormously, to his attractions. His eyes, too, had lost that icy glitter, that domineering look which had been designed to make her tremble in her shoes.

The tense silence seemed to stretch into eons of time before Luke broke it by saying, with what seemed absurdly prosaic casualness, 'You must have seen Kelvin since that day in Marco's *cafeneion?*'

'I have, this morning. He told me he'd seen Litsa every day since they met in the cafe.'

'How did you come to know her?' Luke's voice was edged with a curious inflection that was reflected in his eyes.

Martine bit her lip; this question had not occurred to her and naturally she did not know how to answer it. She still felt contemptuous of her husband for his near indifference about Litsa. He did not appear at all ashamed that Kelvin, a man he disliked intensely, was—or might be—contemplating taking responsibility for a child that was Luke's.

Suddenly she knew a great surge of anger, unreasonable anger since she could not for one moment put her finger on the cause of it. And in her anger she allowed restraint to go by the board, saying what she instantly regretted. 'I went to see her, to find out if what Kelvin said was true. He had told me her child was—was yours.' Martine was very pale now as, from beneath her lashes, she cast her husband an upward glance. She felt desolate, angry with herself because she would far rather Luke had been left in ignorance of her knowledge.

And yet, surely he must have known right from the first that she must one day learn the truth, seeing that Litsa and her little son lived not much more than a mile away.

'You . . . went to ask her if Ulysses is my child?' Luke stared in disbelief, shaking his head from side to side as if he would clear his mind of something unsavoury. 'Martine—!'

'I know how you came by that scar,' she broke in softly. 'It was in a brawl—' She stopped, fiercely catching her lower lip between her teeth. Why was she saying all these things? One look at her husband's dark countenance was more than enough to warn her that he was furiously angry, with that in his expression which seemed to accuse and admonish, and to reveal his contempt for what she had done. She felt guilty without knowing why, and in consequence her own anger rose again. 'Litsa's brothers attacked you and you can't deny it!'

'I don't deny it.' So soft the tone but—oh, heavens, he looked as if he were ready to murder her! Never had she thought to see him in a rage of such intensity. 'What is puzzling me at the moment,' he went on, still in that deceptively smooth and quiet tone, 'is your attitude. Litsa must have told you that—'

'Her child was yours? Yes, of course, she did.' Martine had broken in swiftly as if by so doing she would strengthen her own defence. 'You give her money; you bought the land which she farms.'

'Litsa told you her child was mine?' For the moment his anger had dissolved as he stared at her in total disbelief. 'She actually *told* you—' He stopped, and Martine felt the hairs rise on her forearms as an icy finger traced a line along her spine. Something was wrong. . . . She had known there was but had not been able to put her finger on any clue to the mystery. From that moment when Kelvin, unable to meet her gaze, had told her about Litsa, she had felt that all was not open and above board, that all three—Kelvin, Sophia and Odette—shared a secret that affected her personally. She looked at her husband, saw the anger clearly portrayed in his face again and a quiver of apprehension shot through her. 'You believed what you were told? You actually branded me a rake who would ruin an innocent girl?'

'But—but—' Martine spread her hands in a helpless gesture. 'Isn't it—it true—?' She stepped aside swiftly on noting his expression, her heart pounding so that she actually suffered a physical ache. She saw Luke's eyes glint with fury at her action, knew he was in a towering rage even before he reached her with a silent spring. Taking her unawares and ignoring her high-pitched cry of protest, he gripped her roughly by the shoulders and shook her until her breath seemed to stop and her eyes filled with tears. Only when he saw her distress did he stop. But he could not let go of her because he knew she would fall.

'I hate you!' she whispered fiercely, clenching her small fists as if she would strike him. 'You're a beast! Why should you be angry when you know it's true . . . ?' But she let her voice trail away to silence, catching her breath, trying to release the constriction in her throat, to ease the pain in her chest which had come with the shaking.

'You know now it isn't true, don't you?' he gritted, letting her go when he saw her reach out to grab the rail. 'But you believed it was true until this moment, didn't you? You, my wife, to go and make an inquiry like that! And then, to believe the lies that had been told to you! Believe the worst of your husband! What an opinion you must have of me!' His dark eyes raked her quivering body contemptuously from head to foot. 'Well, I am now under no illusions! I know exactly in what light you regard me—!'

'Luke,' broke in Martine desperately, 'if it isn't true, then why did Litsa say it was?'

'How the devil do I know?' His voice was like a whiplash, his expression still one of the deepest contempt. 'It seems to me there was some sort of conspiracy—' He stopped and his eyes widened. 'Yes, there *was* a conspiracy! You remember when we saw Odette and Kelvin together? We both had the same idea—' He stopped speaking and caught his underlip in a sneer. 'What does it matter? You and I, Martine, are through! I refuse to have anything to do with a woman who could distrust and despise me in the way you have. We shall remain married but it will be a sham.' And on that he turned and left her standing there, by the rail, the one impression in her mind that of bitterness, terrible and soul-searing . . . bitterness on her husband's part. . . .

Martine stood there a long while, her mind in chaos. She had known there was a mystery, but never had it entered her head that both Kelvin and Litsa would tell a lie . . . and yet both had indicated a reluctance to meet her gaze, to look her straight in the eye. For what reason had they lied? And what of Luke's bitterness?

Why should he be bitter? Angry, yes, and perhaps resentful . . . but bitterness was a different thing altogether. Martine's brow creased in thought as she recalled several instances when she had found her husband's behaviour unusual, to say the least. There was that occasion when, after she had made her confession and told him to expect a call from Sophia, he had appeared to be on the verge of saying something important to her. They had been in his study and there had been a tense and expectant moment when she had waited, for he had been so kind and understanding towards her, and instead of encountering anger she had received tenderness. Yes, that particular moment had been tense, but Luke had moved away to the other side of the desk, and as the action was a plain dismissal there had been nothing for Martine to do but obey the silent command and leave his room. Then there had been that moment, that optimistic moment, just a few minutes ago, when she had almost believed him to be jealous.

And now . . . bitterness . . . and hurt. Yes, Luke had been hurt by her distrust; she had seen it in his eyes.

Uncertainty enveloped her; one moment she was certain that her husband loved her, while the next she was telling herself not to be absurd. If he loved her he would never have gone off like he had. On the contrary, he'd have explained . . . or would he? With his pride? She shook her head and told herself emphatically that he would not. She was at fault and he would make her admit it—not only that, but go to him humbly and ask his forgiveness.

It did not take her long to make up her mind, for even though she was not sure that he loved her, she still felt she ought to go to him and say she was sorry for misjudging him. Martine stopped suddenly. If Luke was not the child's father, who was? And why had Litsa's brothers attacked him?

Again her mind was in a whirl of doubt and indecision.

'There's only one solution,' she said aloud. 'I shall make Luke tell me more—explain. After all, I have a right to know what is going on!'

But even as she entered the stting-room where he was standing by the window, Hermes entered and said respectfully, 'You sent for me, Mr. Loukas?'

A flickering glance of indifference came Martine's way before Luke said, 'Go and fetch Litsa Katsellis up here to me.'

The servant's eyes opened wide; they slid from Luke's stern set face to that of Martine. 'Yes, Mr. Loukas.'

'And I want her here at once!'

'Yes—er—shall I take the car?'

'Certainly you shall take the car!'

Martine watched the man depart, closing the door after him. She came forward slowly, but before she could speak Luke said harshly, 'What do you want, Martine?'

She took another step forward, her hands tightly closed at her sides. 'I intended to ask you to explain something to me.'

'Then come back when Litsa arrives.' He flicked an arrogant hand towards the door. 'Meanwhile, I'd like to be alone.'

She went, tears gathering in her eyes at the cold arrogance to which he was subjecting her. The door closed quietly; she went to her bedroom and stood watching the drive, waiting for the car that would bring Litsa up to the villa. So many questions! If Luke was not the father of Ulysses, why had he bought land for the child's mother? And why was he making her an allowance? It was all too much for Martine's bewildered brain and she just sat by the window, waiting.

The car arrived; she watched Hermes open the door to allow the Greek girl to alight and then she rose from the chair and went down to enter the sitting-room just behind Litsa. The girl cast her a frightened glance and went red.

How stern the expression on Luke's face was as he asked, without inviting Litsa to sit down, 'What do you mean by telling my wife that Ulysses is mine?'

'I—I—oh, Mr. Loukas! It was wrong of me! I never forget I hurt Madam Loukas! I tell Kelvin and he say no when I want to come and—and make of the confession.' She lowered her head and started to cry. 'I think God will never forgive me—'

'I asked you a question, Litsa, and you haven't answered it.'

She shook her head, lips quivering. 'Kelvin—he said I must not speak—not tell you—'

'Shall we leave Kelvin out of this?' His voice was so sharp, it made even Martine jump. 'Answer my question, at once!'

'It was Madam Odette and Kelvin—they tell me to say, if your wife ask me, that you are the father of my little Ulysses. They give me—Madam Odette she give me much monies—one thousand drachmae. At first I feel wicked and say I not do this thing, but then she say all the things I can do for my boy with the money, and for my grandmother.'

'Don't I give you enough?' His face was hard as granite. It was easy to guess that his thoughts were mainly on Odette and her diabolical treachery, for Martine now realised why it had been done. They had expected that she, Martine, would instantly leave her husband and ask for a divorce once she learned that her husband's illegitimate child lived so near to her own home. The way would have been clear for both Odette and Kelvin. . . . But things had not worked out the way they had planned. It was a case of 'the best laid plans of mice and men. . . .'

'Yes, Mr. Loukas, you give me much monies and I feel wicked—' The tears came again, in a flood of remorse this time, and Martine, unable to bear the girl's distress, moved towards her, dried her eyes and held her close to her breast.

'Don't cry, Litsa,' she murmured soothingly, stroking the girl's hair. 'It's over and done with now, so there's no need for tears. . . .' Her voice tapered off to silence as she saw her husband's expression. It had softened slightly and his eyes were moving from her face to the delicate white hollow of her throat, then lower, to where Litsa's dark head lay upon Martine's breast.

'Perhaps,' he said with quiet deliberation, 'you will tell my wife who the father of your child was.'

'It was—was your brother—' She lifted her head to seek Martine's eyes. 'I am very sorry to have hurt you, Madam Loukas. It was so wicked and I do not know what made me take the money for something so wrong.'

'Your brother?' Martine stared at Luke, recalling vividly how reluctant she had been to believe that he could act so vilely towards an innocent girl like Litsa. So much was now explained, for although much had become clear in the last few minutes, she had still been puzzled as to why Luke should have given Litsa money.

'Why did Litsa's brothers attack you?' she asked, for at that moment the scar seemed to redden and swell and the nerve she had noticed before began pulsing along its length.

'It was very simple—a case of mistaken identity. My brother and I were the same height and build; it was a very dark night when the attack was made—' He broke off, spreading his hands. 'It's all in the past now, and so there's no profit in talking about it.'

'You fought them all off?' Martine could not help it; she had to know more than he had told her.

'I put up a good show but one had a knife—' Again he broke off, this time because he noticed Litsa's embarrassment, which brought a flow of colour to her cheeks. 'I'll get Hermes to take you home. And let this be a lesson to you, Litsa. Dishonesty will always land you in trouble, and greed is even more evil. I hope you understand what I am saying?'

She nodded, avoiding his gaze. 'I will never do anything like this again.' She moved towards the door, and again tears filled her eyes. 'Kelvin was in love with me, but now that I have not done as he told me I think he will be angry and leave me.'

'Kelvin shall be told that I made you confess.'

Litsa dabbed her eyes with the handkerchief she had forgotten to return to its owner. 'Will you? Oh, that is very kind, Mr. Loukas! Perhaps Kelvin will not go away and leave me after all.'

Martine looked at her, taking in the girl's beautiful classical features, and she said gently after awhile, 'I am sure, Litsa dear, that Kelvin still loves you and that you will be inviting us all to a wedding before very long.'

'Oh. . . .' breathed Litsa. 'It is good of you to say so. . . .'

Luke had already rung the bell and at that moment Hermes came into the room. Litsa said goodbye and left. Martine watched the door close, then looked across the room to where her husband stood with his back to the window. Beyond him was the broad slope leading down to the Sanctuary, and the vista of olives and forest trees with the shimmering river flowing gently, its surface in the sunlight like silver tinted with gold. Closer still was the kaleidoscope of colour and form which made the villa grounds so enchanting. Birds and butterflies flitted about among the flowers and trees and all was so peaceful that it seemed like sacrilege for her and Luke to be standing here, both tensed. And on his part hostility was undisguisedly portrayed in the set of his mouth, the tautness of his jaw, the glitter of anger and contempt in his eyes.

Martine knew that if this situation was to be resolved she would have to accept that she must be the one to make the advances . . . and to persist in spite of possible rejections. For Luke was so proud! Like an ancient Greek god, he stood looking at her as if in judgement, with condemnation in his eyes and nothing else. He would not meet her half-way, she thought, but suddenly she knew she could not humble herself too much; she would draw the line at going down on her knees to him, even figuratively!

She moved forward and said, in soft and steady tones, 'Luke—I'm sorry for misjudging you. In my own defence I do want to say that when Kelvin first told me what you had done to Litsa I refused to believe it and did say that someone else must be the father—'

'Are you making excuses?' with a sort of icy contempt in his voice. 'If so, you can save your breath.'

She bit her lip and persevered. 'I was merely stating a fact. There is no excuse. In any case, I should have come to you—'

'I cannot understand why you didn't.'

'Kelvin said—'

'Kelvin! My heavens, woman, don't you think I've heard enough of him?'

'—that you would tell me to mind my own business, that what you had done before our marriage had nothing to do with me, and I had to admit that you would be very likely to adopt that attitude.' She continued as if the interruption had never been made, continued in the face of the rising anger which her husband made no attempt to disguise. 'That was the reason I went to Litsa instead. She told me you were the father—'

'And you were by then only too ready to believe it. So much so that you agreed to leave me and go away with Kelvin!' He came closer now and she could scarcely refrain from stepping back, an action which she knew for sure would only serve to add fuel to the fire of his wrath. 'You'd have broken up our marriage on flimsy evidence like that? Well, as I said before, I now know where I stand.'

She looked at him, noting the inflexibility of his features, the throbbing, uncontrollable pulsing of the scar, the lean brown hands clenched tightly at his sides. More than anything, though, she took notice of the expression in his eyes. . . .

She said quietly, 'If we love each other, Luke, then surely forgiveness is a vital part of it. I'm admitting I was wrong and asking you to forgive me. . . .' Her voice faltered to a stop as he came very close, to tower above her, the bitterness and pain that had been in his eyes giving place to the dark embers of fury.

'If we *love* each other! What the devil are you talking about? Do you suppose for one moment I could be in love with a woman who does not trust me—who was ready to run away because she believed the lies that had been spoken about me?'

She met his savage gaze unflinchingly as she made one last bid for happiness. 'Perhaps you will not believe me, Luke, but the reason I had decided to leave you had nothing whatsoever to do with the lies you mention. I was leaving because I had discovered I loved you.' She paused, but he did not speak; he just stared down into her eyes, eyes misted with tears, eyes too big for the small, pale face that was raised anxiously to his. 'I believe you love me now—in fact, I have begun to wonder just when you began to love me. I feel we have both held back things we ought to have revealed.'

He still said nothing and after a long silence she continued with a hint of despair, 'I can't humble myself any further, Luke. I have my pride as well as you. I ask you to forgive me and if—if you won't m–meet me half-way—No, I knew from the first that you'd not do that, but I also knew the limits of my own humility as well.' Her eyes were bright with tears but there was a certain element of pride in them, too, which could not possibly escape his notice. 'I've said I love you, without being *quite* certain that you love me—because you haven't told me that you do. I agreed to go away with Kelvin but I know that, even had you agreed to a divorce, I'd never have married him. He was very angry when I confessed that it was you I loved; he said I'd been willing to use him and I suppose his accusations were justified.'

She stopped and waited, despair gathering and increasing with every second that passed. Then suddenly his whole demeanour changed—his eyes softened, his mouth relaxed and his hands came slowly out to take hers, eagerly, thankfully given. She wept on his breast, wept uncontrollably in relief, for she had been afraid, terribly afraid that his arrogant Greek background would prevail and pride would ruin both their lives. He produced a handkerchief and tenderly dabbed at her eyes, but it eventually took a stern word and a threat to have any effect in stemming her tears.

'It's—reaction,' she quivered. 'Luke, oh, please let me hear you say it!'

But he kissed her first and then said softly, his mouth moist and tender against her cheek, 'I love you, my own darling wife.'

'And you forgive me?'

To her surprise he paused, and then, unexpectedly, 'I think that it is I who must ask forgiveness, my dear. I was so proud, and hurt. I saw again the wrong a woman had done me and I believed I could make myself hate you—hate you so much that I'd never want to come near you again. But I had no intention of ending the marriage—' He was stopped by a tender finger on his lips and he smiled then as he looked with deep love and tenderness into her eyes. 'You're quite right, my dearest love. It is all in the past. We were the victims of a vicious plot and we've emerged triumphant so—yes, beloved, I agree with you that it's all best forgotten.'

His lips were gentle yet strong with passion as they met hers and for a long while there was total silence in the room. Martine was breathless when at last he held her from him, regarding her flushed face at arms' length, his eyes travelling to her hair, which was dishevelled to say the least.

'No, dearest,' he said with some amusement as he noticed her expression, 'don't ask me when I started to love you because I could not answer. I felt a deep attraction from the first, but with the lesson of Odette ever in my mind I had no intention of running any risks again. I told myself I did not believe in love between a man and a woman.'

'You told *me* that, too,' she reminded him and he gave her a playful shake. 'Well, I can't help feeling rather clever!' she added and received another shake for her trouble. 'But you believe in it now,' she said confidently, 'and you always will, dearest Luke, because I will never ever let you down.'

'Nor I you, beloved,' was his fervent response and as he drew her close to his heart they both knew without any doubts at all that their love, born in this realm of the pagan gods and heroes of long, long ago, would endure in the same way that the memories of Olympia had done . . . forever.

Silhouette Romance

IT'S YOUR OWN SPECIAL TIME

Contemporary romances for today's women.
Each month, six very special love stories will be yours
from SILHOUETTE. Look for them wherever books are sold
or order now from the coupon below.

$1.50 each

Hampson	☐ 1 ☐ 4 ☐ 16 ☐ 27 ☐ 28 ☐ 40 ☐ 52 ☐ 64 ☐ 94	Browning	☐ 12 ☐ 38 ☐ 53 ☐ 73 ☐ 93
Stanford	☐ 6 ☐ 25 ☐ 35 ☐ 46 ☐ 58 ☐ 88	Michaels	☐ 15 ☐ 32 ☐ 61 ☐ 87
		John	☐ 17 ☐ 34 ☐ 57 ☐ 85
Hastings	☐ 13 ☐ 26 ☐ 44 ☐ 67	Beckman	☐ 8 ☐ 37 ☐ 54 ☐ 72 ☐ 96
Vitek	☐ 33 ☐ 47 ☐ 66 ☐ 84		

$1.50 each

☐ 3 Powers	☐ 29 Wildman	☐ 56 Trent	☐ 79 Halldorson
☐ 5 Goforth	☐ 30 Dixon	☐ 59 Vernon	☐ 80 Stephens
☐ 7 Lewis	☐ 31 Halldorson	☐ 60 Hill	☐ 81 Roberts
☐ 9 Wilson	☐ 36 McKay	☐ 62 Hallston	☐ 82 Dailey
☐ 10 Caine	☐ 39 Sinclair	☐ 63 Brent	☐ 83 Hallston
☐ 11 Vernon	☐ 41 Owen	☐ 69 St. George	☐ 86 Adams
☐ 14 Oliver	☐ 42 Powers	☐ 70 Afton Bonds	☐ 89 James
☐ 19 Thornton	☐ 43 Robb	☐ 71 Ripy	☐ 90 Major
☐ 20 Fulford	☐ 45 Carroll	☐ 74 Trent	☐ 92 McKay
☐ 21 Richards	☐ 48 Wildman	☐ 75 Carroll	☐ 95 Wisdom
☐ 22 Stephens	☐ 49 Wisdom	☐ 76 Hardy	☐ 97 Clay
☐ 23 Edwards	☐ 50 Scott	☐ 77 Cork	☐ 98 St. George
☐ 24 Healy	☐ 55 Ladame	☐ 78 Oliver	☐ 99 Camp

$1.75 each

☐ 100 Stanford	☐ 104 Vitek	☐ 108 Hampson	☐ 112 Stanford
☐ 101 Hardy	☐ 105 Eden	☐ 109 Vernon	☐ 113 Browning
☐ 102 Hastings	☐ 106 Dalley	☐ 110 Trent	☐ 114 Michaels
☐ 103 Cork	☐ 107 Bright	☐ 111 South	☐ 115 John
	☐ 116 Lindley	☐ 117 Scott	

Introducing
First Love from Silhouette
Romances for teenage girls to build their dreams on.

They're wholesome, fulfilling, supportive novels about every young girl's dreams. Filled with the challenges, excitement— and responsibilities—of love's first blush, *First Love* paperbacks prepare young adults to stand at the threshold of maturity with confidence and composure.

Introduce your daughter, or some young friend to the *First Love* series by giving her a one-year subscription to these romantic originals, written by leading authors. She'll receive two NEW $1.75 romances each month, a total of 24 books a year. Send in your coupon now. **There's nothing quite as special as a First Love.**

Silhouette Romance

15-Day Free Trial Offer
6 Silhouette Romances

6 Silhouette Romances, free for 15 days! We'll send you 6 new Silhouette Romances to keep for 15 days, absolutely free! If you decide not to keep them, send them back to us. You pay nothing.

Free Home Delivery. But if you enjoy them as much as we think you will, keep them by paying the invoice enclosed with your free trial shipment. We'll pay all shipping and handling charges. You get the convenience of Home Delivery and we pay the postage and handling charge each month.

Don't miss a copy. The Silhouette Book Club is the way to make sure you'll be able to receive every new romance we publish before they're sold out. There is no minimum number of books to buy and you can cancel at any time.

This offer expires June 30, 1982